PRAIS

Short, sweet, and scary - I would recommend this book as the perfect bedtime story, so long as you don't sleep near an attic and you don't mind a few spooky ghosts haunting your dreams!

KRISTIANA SFIRLEA, AUTHOR OF LEGEND OF THE STORM SNEEZER

Spooky little gem of a read. Just the right amount of things that go bump in the night. I enjoyed the wholesome characters in a sinister plot.

HOPE, GOODREADS

This is a great story for younger kids that want something creepy/scary but not necessarily nightmare inducing. The Goosebumps series and the Fear Street series come to mind for comparison.

AMAZON CUSTOMER

FAKE NORA
KELLY MARTIN

MONSTER IVY
PUBLISHING

Cover design by Cammie Larsen

Cover image from shutterstock.com

To everyone who walks by mirrors quickly.

CHAPTER ONE

The sign read DO NOT TOUCH.

Twelve-year-old Nora Williams folded her arms, staring at the sign. Electricity flowed through her fingers … not really … she wasn't a superhero or anything. She was a bored girl in a boring store with her (sometimes) boring mother. It was Saturday morning, and instead of sleeping in like a lot of her friends got to do or fishing like her brother was doing with her dad right now, she was stuck in an antique store with her mama. Oh … joy.

Nora's mama loved old things: names, places, objects. That's why Nora's name was Nora. There were no other Noras in her class. In fact, the only other Noras were great grandparents of her classmates. Nora enjoyed being unique, though, so she didn't hate her name. She hated being in the antique store at way too early o'clock on Saturday, and she hated the sign that said not to touch.

The only thing she liked about the antique stores were the stories she could make up about the objects inside. Nora loved using her imagination, and antique stores created the perfect location to let her mind go wild with all sorts of fun situations to pass the time.

This particular antique store was a new one for her mama. The building had been an old house at one time, with two stories, beaten up white wood on the outside, and a sign at the top that said GIBSON'S ANTIQUES in big letters.

Inside, there were signs posted everywhere. They didn't want you to touch the old four-post bed, the old bathtub, the old razor, the old dishes, the old tables, the old chairs, the old high chair, the old posters, the … old … everything …

And Nora had just about had it with all the ordering signs. She knew not to touch things. She wasn't a baby. Her mother had dragged her to antique shops her entire life. She knew what she could and could not touch and had always kept her hands to herself.

Except …

The pull of the sign drew her in ... Maybe not the sign, maybe what it was plastered over. She'd already looked around the store twenty times. Her mother was on the lookout for one particular piece of ... something ... Nora's mama had probably told her, but Nora hadn't paid attention, and this was the fourth store that day they'd visited to find whatever it was her mama had her eye on.

Nora had looked around restlessly until she found herself in the back corner of the store, in a little hallway that had dim lights, a musty smell, and dust on the antique pieces, which was unusual because Nora had seen her share of antique stores. Even though the things were old, the pieces inside them were usually dust-free. Maybe that's why she was drawn to this part of the store, because it was quite unlike anything she'd seen before.

There were a few stuffed animals in the little hallway—taxidermized stuffed. A tricycle sat discarded on the floor, making Nora's mind run wild with the image of a small boy riding it down an old dirt road. In her mind, the boy was being chased by a deer whose head was mounted on the wall. The boy was going faster and faster, as did the deer. Until the boy flipped off and landed on his bottom, looking up at the deer and yelling as the deer attacked.

The electricity buzzed in Nora's fingertips as the story faded from her mind. Guess she'd never know what happened to that boy, not that he was real. Her friends said she was too old to play pretend or disappear into make-believe worlds, so Nora normally kept that part of her life to herself. Still, when she was alone, her mind wandered no matter how much she tried to stop it.

At the end of the long, narrow hallway stood a rather unimpressive—to Nora—dresser and mirror. The dresser was a medium tone wood with two drawers on the bottom. The top section was divided into two separate drawers. Tarnished handles were on each section. On top of the dresser, stood a tall oval mirror with ornate, curved wood carvings all around it—well as much as Nora could see around it anyway. A yellowed cloth covering laid over the mirror, keeping her from seeing her reflection. It didn't bother Nora any. She didn't care to look at her fiery red hair and freckles anyway.

Still … the sign read DO NOT TOUCH, and Nora's fingers itched to touch it. She wouldn't linger. She'd touch it for a second, then back away. It would be easy, quick, painless, and it would show the store owner that no one told Nora Williams what to do.

She'd never felt that way before about anything: defiant, practically angry that she couldn't touch the dresser and mirror. It was unfair, and what Nora disliked most in this world was unfairness.

With a buzzing radiating from the bottoms of her feet to the tips of her fingers, Nora slowly reached for the mirror. No one was back here. Nora doubted they even had cameras watching her. One quick touch … that's all it would take for the strong pull to end.

Her mind practically hummed the closer her fingers got to the dresser. The closer she got, the stronger the pull amplified, the more she wanted to touch it … needed to touch it. No, she needed to pull the covering from over the mirror. She needed to see the reflection.

Needed!

Nora's hand practically shook as her fingers crept toward the fabric. Almost there … Almost …

"What are you doing!" A loud, male voice boomed behind her. Nora jumped and put her hands in her pockets. When she turned, she saw a tall man with a gut the size of her Uncle Jude's and suspenders holding up his jeans. He had a scowl on his reddening face, and sweat beaded on his temples.

Nora tried to think of an explanation. Why would she touch something that said not to touch … she had to think and think fast. Before she could even think of an excuse, her mother peered around the tall giant of a man.

Her mother, Rita Shoemake-Williams, stepped around the giant and smiled at Nora. "There you are, sweetie. I've been looking for you." And Nora knew that was more than likely the truth. Honestly, her mother loved their girl trips to antique stores. She thought they were bonding. Nora didn't hate the bonding part. She liked spending time with her mother, but she absolutely hated old things—not that she'd ever tell her mother. It would break her heart.

"Sorry, I got carried away looking at your beautiful pieces." Nora grinned from ear to ear, trying her best to sound sincere.

"Uh-huh." The tall giant's eyes narrowed. "You sure you weren't touching things you weren't supposed to?"

Nora shook her head, adamant that it wasn't the case. She wasn't one to lie, but this seemed an appropriate time.

Her mother's long, off-white, bohemian-style skirt swished against the floor as she made her way over to Nora. Her long, curly red hair fell over her shoulders. "Oh my! Nora, you've found it!"

"I have?"

"Yes! Oh, don't be so modest, my sweet girl. You found exactly what I was looking for. Dresser with oval mirror. Ornate. Wood not too dark, not too light. Sturdy. I'll take it."

Her mother reached for the mirror covering before the tall, giant man yelled at her to stop. Guess children weren't the only ones not supposed to touch things in the store. "You can't have that one."

"Why not?" her mother asked, nearly flabbergasted.

"Why not?" the tall giant fumbled for words. "Because … because it's defective."

"How can it be defective? It literally is a mirror and dresser."

"I mean … it's … it needs work. And it's not for sale. I can't sell that one."

"Why?"

"Because I can't."

"It's in your store," Mama reminded him.

"In the back of my store," he corrected.

"But it's exactly what I want."

He narrowed his eyes. "Do you actually know what you want? It's always such a difficult thing to know what one wants ..."

"Mr. Gibson, why won't you let me buy this dresser?"

The tall giant, Mr. Gibson, wiped the sweat from his brow. "Because ... I promised my mother I'd never sell it. It has ... issues."

Mama pulled out her wallet. "I'll pay triple the asking price."

Mr. Gibson's eyes lit up. "Ma will understand. Probably a silly superstition anyway. Come with me, Ma'am. I'll ring you up."

Mama nodded with a smirk at Nora as she followed Mr. Gibson to the front to buy the dresser. All alone again, she turned toward the mirror, glad it's coming home with them.

A sound caught Nora's attention, the sound of a girl laughing from somewhere far away. She felt bad for her. Nora bet she was trapped in this store just like she was.

Nora sent up thoughts of solidarity and made her way toward her mother at the front, not seeing another single soul in the store.

CHAPTER TWO

Nora's father, Chris, and her younger brother, Nolan, arrived back at home around the same time as Nora and her mother, which was good for them, because it had taken three people to load the dresser into the truck at the antique store. Nora had no idea how the two of them were going to get it in their house, but when she saw her father's truck there, she smiled, as did her mother. "Looks like we'll get some help after all," Nora's mother said.

"From Daddy, yeah. I have bigger muscles than Nolan." It wasn't a slight or offhand remark about Nolan. It was, in fact, true. Nolan was five years old and, as most five-year-olds, was stick thin and had the muscle mass of a green bean. It wasn't a mean thing to say, though Nora would never say it to

Nolan's face. They didn't get along all the time, but she would never hurt him on purpose.

"For now." Nora's mother grinned as she pulled their truck into the driveway. She slowed to a stop and rolled down her window. "Catch anything?" she asked, referring to fish. If Chris Williams was off on Saturday, he fished, and most of the time, he took Nolan with him. He would have taken Nora, if she wanted, and a few times she had gone. As much as she didn't like antique malls, she did prefer them to fishing, which wasn't saying much.

"A few." Her father picked up a tackle box and two rods from the back of his truck. Nolan bounced around in the yard, fighting an imaginary enemy with a stick. "Nolan caught more than me."

"You don't say." Rita laughed, watching her boy in the yard playing happily. Nora watched him, too. It would be nice to be young and free like Nolan again. Other times, she loved being twelve. Twelve meant she was close to being an adult, and that's what she had always wanted to be.

Her mother turned off the ignition and climbed out of the truck. "So … I need you to help me with something."

Chris turned to face her. "Oh?"

"Yeah, it's in the back of the truck. I finally

found it!" She practically jumped up and down from excitement. She was where Nolan got his bouncy demeanor from. Nora and her dad were both a little more put together, a little more polished. Her mama and Nolan were, what her grandmother called, flower children, aka they lived a little freer than anyone else.

"Your favorite china pattern?" Chris looked bewildered.

"No, silly. That was last week. I found the dresser and mirror I've been looking for. You know that new place down on Olive Street? Well, they had it. I paid a little too much for it, but it's beautiful and perfect for the guest room!" She clapped her hands wildly as Nora's dad opened his mouth to say something.

With a shake of his head and a grin on his face, he simply smiled back. "Let me put this fishing equipment up, and I'll help you."

"Deal." Her mother kissed him on the cheek and gave Nora a thumbs-up sign as her dad went to the garage to put his fishing gear away.

"Nora, come here!" Nolan called from the front yard. She shook her head and did as he asked. His excitement about things could be contagious at times.

"So, you caught fish, huh?" Nora asked as Nolan kicked a soccer ball across the yard.

"A few. Daddy mostly. Wanna play?" He kicked the ball with his left foot, then his right.

Did she want to play? No. Not really. Would she? "Get out there as far as you can, okay?"

Nolan grinned from ear to ear as he ran to the far end of the yard, about a small soccer field away. Nora kicked her old soccer ball as hard as she could, thinking it would go over her little brother's head. Instead, he jumped up and caught it. A huge smile was plastered on his face when his feet hit the ground.

Nora was impressed. "Great job, Kid. We're gonna have to change your nickname to Kangaroo."

"Nah, I like Kid."

"Me too."

Nolan kicked the ball back. It was a great big kick that Nora had to run to get. She got ready to kick it back when her mother asked them to help move the dresser. "We'll play later," Nora promised.

About an hour later, the dresser and mirror stood in the guest room at the back of the house. Nora had never understood why they had a guest room. They rarely had guests except for her grandmother, who stayed every so often. But this room was the room her mama put all of her antique treasures in. It was the room that, as she told Nora, she could express herself fully. The room was painted an off-white, nearly pale-yellow color with thick gold drapes hanging from floor to ceiling. The drapes had plum and scarlet-colored flowers on them, which matched the bedspread on the antique bed. Four tall posts circled the bed, each with spiral poles that became thinner from base to ceiling. The room also had an old rocking chair where everyone had been forbidden to sit, in case it decided to fall, and an old baby crib with an incredibly ugly porcelain doll inside. Nora could never look at that doll when she went into the room. Ever. It freaked her out with its too-pale skin and too-black eyes. On the far end of the room sat the newly acquired dresser with the mirror on top. Her father took great care in helping her mother move the piece in, setting it up just right so it wouldn't tip over, and attaching the mirror on top. Because they didn't want the mirror to break, they had left the covering on top of it. The yellowing fabric fit in with the room, and Nora thought maybe they should just leave it on forever.

Her mother had other ideas. "One last thing …" she pulled the cloth off the mirror, which was a bit of an anti-climactic moment. Nora didn't know what she'd been expecting, really, with the build-up from the man at the store, and then the final mirror reveal, but it was … just a mirror. A faded, old mirror at that with dirt lines falling like tears from the top of the oval to the bottom. The edges had a warped effect like something out of a funhouse. When Nora looked at her reflection for the slightest of seconds, something felt off. It wasn't like looking in her bathroom mirror where she saw herself in color, just as she figured she looked in real life. This mirror distorted her just so she appeared not herself entirely.

That same electricity that had filled her at the antique store started at her toes once more, rising up from her legs and through the top of her head. If anyone else in her family noticed it, they never said a word. Nolan had already gotten bored with all things mirrors and ran out of the room with his stick and imaginary opponent. Her father was already putting his tools away, and her mother wiped the dust off the dresser and appraised the mirror glass. "Well, it's more worn than I would have liked, but it will do. Nothing a little elbow grease won't fix." She left the room, Nora figured to get some "elbow grease"—whatever that was. With everyone else busy, Nora felt the pull to look at her reflection growing. Knowing that it was just a mirror, and a mirror couldn't do anything bad, she walked up to the dresser and stared at her reflection.

The reflection stared back.

Nora was one of the shortest in sixth grade, and the mirror showed that. All she could see was from her shoulders, up. The rest of her body was too short to reflect. The dirt tears on the glass ran down her reflection, giving it the effect of blood running down her face. The warped glass made her face curvy, unnaturally angled. Nora stared at her reflection, unable to look away, as the tingly feeling ran from her toes to the tip of her head and back again.

A swift movement behind her caught her attention, and she quickly turned, noticing nothing that could have made such a movement. Her father had already left, and she was alone in the room, alone with her reflection.

When Nora turned back toward the mirror, she thought the reflection smirked. But that couldn't have happened. Reflections only did what the person did, and she most certainly hadn't smirked.

Suddenly feeling like she wanted out of the room, Nora turned and practically ran, not looking back when she heard the faintest sound of something hitting glass.

CHAPTER THREE

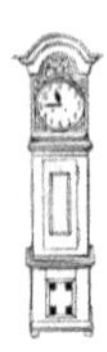

The rest of the day, Nora didn't think much about the dresser and mirror. She convinced herself that what she'd seen was a trick of the light, and her smirk in the reflection was simply the way the glass of the mirror was messed up. Once her mother cleaned it and restored it, everything would be back to normal once more.

After supper, she watched television with her mother while her father worked in the garage, and her brother put a puzzle together. Every so often, Nora noticed he'd look into space, occasionally laughing at some joke no one else heard or understood. Little brothers were weird, Nora decided and continued watching the show with her mother until it was time for bed.

Rita tucked Nolan in his bed first. Nolan's room was across the hall from Nora's. With their doors open, Nora could hear the story her mother told him. It was the one about the Three Billy Goats Gruff and the troll who lived under the bridge. Nora would never admit it now at the mature age of twelve, but that story was one of her favorites. The way the goats practically set their brothers up to be eaten by the troll only for the troll to be carried away by the water at the end was brilliant. Nora rolled over on her side and pretended to sleep while her mother's soft, soothing voice echoed through her room as well.

A few minutes later, her mama came into her room. "Sleeping, Nora?"

Nora decided to pretend to wake up, so her mother didn't know she liked hearing her read those baby stories to her brother. "I was." She fake yawned. "Did you tuck Nolan in?"

"I did. He loves that story about the goats, you know?"

"Does he?" she asked, knowing full well that he did.

"Ready to read your chapter book with me?" Nora's mama had started reading a chapter of a book every night to Nora before bed. Nora loved it nearly as much as she loved hearing Nolan's stories.

She nodded, and her mother grabbed the book they were currently reading. She crawled into bed with Nora, who snuggled against her mother. The soft, soothing sounds of her mama reading lulled Nora's eyes shut, and before she knew it, she was fast asleep.

The scratching woke Nora up.

Or she thought it was scratching. Once she thought about it, the sound—the squeak followed by a thud—sounded like the sound she'd heard in the guest room earlier. Nora wiped her eyes as she sat up in her bed. The only light in the room was from a security light outside her window that let in a little light, which Nora had always loved. A tall tree outside her window made weird shadows dance across her walls, especially when the wind blew. The wind was blowing that night. Thunder clapped overhead.

A storm was coming.

Nora pulled her covers closer to her as the squeak—thud, squeak—thud, continued to sound from the guest room down the hallway. She knew she had a few choices: lie down, cover up, and go back to sleep; sit there and listen to all the sounds, wondering where they were coming from; get her parents and have them think she was a baby like Nolan; or investigate the sounds herself.

Without much thought, Nora settled on the first choice: lie down, cover her head, and go back to sleep. Nora wasn't the kind of person who would check to see what a sound was. She was an ignore-it-and-it-would-go-away type. So, that's what she did. She covered her head and tried her best to go back to sleep.

But the sound continued.

Squeak.

Thud.

Squeak.

Thud.

Squeak.

Thud.

All through the night, until Nora couldn't take it anymore. Could her parents not hear it? Sure, their room was on the first floor, but the sound was so loud, she knew they should have been able to hear it. And what about Nolan? Was he in his room listening? Was he scared? She hoped he wasn't scared. He got on her nerves sometimes, but she never wanted him scared at all.

Her thoughts centered on her brother and if he

was scared or not. She tried calling his name but got no answer from him. Resigned to the fact that she needed to be a good big sister and check on her little brother, Nora reluctantly rolled out of her covers and placed her feet on the cold, hardwood floor. The sudden shock of coldness made her recoil, and it took everything she had not to jump back under her covers.

The grandfather clock downstairs chimed three times to let her know it was three in the morning. She'd check on Nolan quickly, make sure he was okay, then run back under her covers. It was simple and easy as that.

She took a deep breath and counted to three before running through her door and across the hallway to Nolan's room. She paused at the doorway, listening. It took a couple of seconds, but finally, she was greeted with the soft sounds of Nolan breathing in his sleep. Relief washed over Nora now that she knew her brother was okay. She laughed at herself for how scared she'd been and made her way back across the hallway to her room. Before she got halfway across the hallway, the electric feeling started against her toes again. The tingly sensation caught her off guard, and she tried to run back into her room and put her feet on the bed. She couldn't move, though. She was stuck in the middle of the dark hallway, unable to do anything but stand there and allow the tingles from electricity flow through her.

Squeak.

Thud.

Squeak.

Thud.

The sounds came faster and faster, louder and louder. Should she wake up Nolan and have him investigate the sounds with her? It would make her feel better, but he was only five. What could a five-year-old face besides an imaginary friend?

The fear inside her didn't ease up, but she found herself walking toward the guest room. Wait, no, not exactly walking. She wasn't walking. It was more like being dragged, only of her own accord. She couldn't explain it. She didn't want to walk to the guest room, but she felt her own feet move and knew she was the one doing it. She stopped at the open door to the room and forced herself to stop. There was nothing inside of her that wanted to check on the sound or the room. Her brother was okay. That was all that mattered, and the sound was more than likely an animal of some kind. A mouse, perhaps?

Nora decided then and there to run back to her room and cover her head up. She'd been brave enough for the time being. She checked on her brother and should be proud of what she'd accomplished. But her feet wouldn't move anywhere except straight ahead.

So, since she had no other options, ahead she went. Since the room was at the back of the house and had no streetlights shining in, she flipped on the light as she entered. Not surprisingly, the room looked exactly as it had when she'd left earlier: gold curtains drawn, comforter on the bed, dresser and mirror sitting in the same place …

Except the mirror had tilted down slightly so the reflection showed more of the floor than the other side of the room.

Nora felt foolish. Of course the squeak, thud was the mirror on the dresser, but not in the paranormal way! The mirror and dresser were old, very old. Gravity on top of old metal had caused the mirror to tilt downward, which made the squeak, thud sound. Why had it happened over and over? Maybe the age of the mirror and hinges had something to do with that as well. Relieved, Nora laughed at herself and shut off the light.

"Nora." She heard her name whispered from

inside the room. The hairs on the back of her neck stood up.

It had to be in her imagination. Just as Nolan had recently gotten an imaginary friend, Nora now had an active imagination. That had to be it, especially at three in the morning.

Squeak.

Thud.

Nora jumped at the sound but didn't leave the room. Something was wrong in here. Very wrong. She needed to figure out what it was, then run and tell her parents. If there was something wrong with the mirror, they needed to know so they could take it back.

Nora.

This time she heard her name practically in her head, not like a solid voice, but as a memory, a sound echoing through her skull.

Nora turned, berating her imagination for getting the best of her. She was twelve years old! She shouldn't be afraid of anything, and ghosts didn't exist. At all.

To prove to herself that she wasn't a scaredy-cat, Nora decided to go and face her newly formed fear of the mirror. With the electricity and the tingling running up and down her body, she ran to the mirror and flipped it where her reflection could be seen.

Thunder erupted outside.

Her reflection smiled.

Nora did not.

CHAPTER FOUR

Nora woke up in her bed. She sat up and rubbed her eyes, wiping away the fogginess from the night before. How had she gotten back in her bed? What time was it?

As if on cue, the grandfather clock downstairs rang eight times, letting her know it was eight o'clock. Normally, she slept a little later, but that morning she didn't feel much like it. She stretched and waited for the smell of bacon and eggs, the meal her mother always cooked on Sunday mornings.

She waited … and she waited …

No fabulous smells of bacon and eggs wafted through her door. In fact, she didn't hear anything, either. It wasn't like the night before, where she heard so many noises. This quiet was almost deafening.

No birds sang outside.

The tree didn't beat on her window.

In fact, it didn't move at all.

The room was filled with a dull gray to let her know that the clouds outside hadn't dissipated, and the sun wouldn't come out for a while. That was fine. Nora didn't hate the dull gray. What she hated was the unnatural silence. Why was it so quiet?

She put her feet on the floor, which wasn't warm and wasn't cold. She walked to her door and realized once she got there that she hadn't heard her footsteps. Curious, she went to her brother's room across the hallway to see if he was awake. His room sat just as it had the night before, only the bed was perfectly made. The shelves were neatly arranged with all his toys up where Mama loved for them to be, but they rarely were. It looked like a child's bedroom, but a child's bedroom that had never been used.

"Nolan?" Nora whispered, unsure where he would have gone. He never made his bed by himself, so her mother had to have come up there and got him dressed for the day and made the bed.

If that was the case, why hadn't she woken Nora up as well?

Nora left Nolan's room and headed down the stairs to the living room area. The steps made no sound, which Nora was getting used to. Once on the bottom landing, she turned to the left and saw her living room and kitchen exactly as it should look, except, just as in Nolan's room, it appeared immaculate. It was clean, neat, orderly. The books on the bookshelf in the living room were lined up in perfect rows. No dust fell upon them. The rug in the living room was the same purple and teal one she was accustomed to, but the grape juice stain Nolan had created a few months ago was gone now.

In the kitchen, the chairs were pushed in perfectly, cabinets closed, dishes out of the sink. If Nora didn't know better, she'd think she'd stepped into one of those home ads in a magazine. Only those weren't real. They were staged. Her house was real. While her mother did clean regularly, there was always something lying around that should have been lying around. Not this morning. There was nothing.

Deciding she needed her mama, Nora ran back where she came and went straight at the steps toward her parents' room. She knocked on the door and listened, hearing nothing from inside. She knocked again. Nothing. Harder and harder, she pounded, begging in her mind for her mother to answer. She needed her so badly to tell her that everything was okay, and it was all a misunderstanding.

When the door didn't open after five minutes of banging, Nora got scared and pushed the door open herself.

Just like Nolan's room, her parents' was immaculately cleaned and decorated. Their bed was made, clothes tidy, closet impeccable. It was a room in a sterile house about to be sold.

So why did it look like this now?

"Mama!" Nora yelled, expecting an echo throughout the room. "Mama!" Frantic that her mother might have, for some reason, slept in the guest room last night, Nora forgot her fear and ran up the steps. She didn't stop until she reached the second-floor landing. Out of breath, she continued to the end of the hallway and pushed the guest room door open. The only thing Nora could think of was maybe her parents decided to change rooms on a whim and moved to the antique guest room. Her mother would have loved it. Her father, not so much.

Once she got to the door, she froze.

The room looked exactly as it had before: gold curtains drawn, comforter on the bed, dresser and mirror sitting in the same place. It hadn't changed a bit. Then why had all the other rooms?

Slowly, Nora walked to the mirror, which was bent toward the ground again. It was silly, at this moment, to be mesmerized by a mirror, but that's what was happening.

Nora lifted it and saw the reflection inside.

It was the same room she occupied, of course. That's what mirrors did, they reflected what they saw. Nothing more. Nothing less.

And yet …

The hair on her arms stood on end, and it took everything she had not to yell … not that she could yell if given the opportunity.

The reflection in the mirror was the same as the room she currently stood in: same bed, same bookshelf, same golden curtains, same golden color on the walls. Everything matched, except for one thing: Nora's reflection didn't stare back at her.

In fact, her reflection stood in the doorway of the room, watching Nora curiously. Nora rubbed her eyes, knowing it had to be some kind of dream. She blinked a few times, and nothing in the reflection changed. She looked behind her, and there was nothing there. Not even her shadow.

She pinched her arm, and nothing changed in the reflection. Same room. Same Nora. Different location. Her reflection tilted her head and smiled ever so slightly at Nora, making her stomach hurt. Knowing she needed to wake up as soon as possible, Nora pinched her arm harder, so hard she knew it would leave a mark. A mark was fine. A mark meant everything was back to normal.

She blinked a few times, expecting to be back in her bed.

The scene in front of her didn't change.

"Nora, what are you doing up this time of night?" Her mother asked, or rather she heard her mother's voice. It sounded like it came from inside the mirror. That wasn't right, though. She was in the real world, not the reflection.

Her mother showed up in the doorway of the reflection and placed her hand on Nora's other self in the doorway. "Nora, everything alright?"

Quickly, Nora turned behind her to see her mother and tell her that it most certainly wasn't okay. Her mama wasn't there. No one was there in the doorway.

"Nora, honey?" Her mama asked again from the

other side of the mirror. Terror gripped Nora, and she started beating on the glass to get her mother's attention.

"I'm right here, Mama! Right here!" Her mother never looked in her direction. Only smiled down at Nora's reflection, at Fake Nora.

"I'm fine." Fake Nora peered at Nora in the mirror, their eyes met, and Fake Nora smiled from ear to ear. "Everything is perfect now."

"No! Mama!" Nora beat the mirror harder and harder, praying that her mother would hear her and get her out, at the very least wake her up, or, at the very, very least, not listen to the Fake Nora. She had to know that wasn't her, right? A mother had to know her own daughter?

"Good. Now, let's get you back to bed." Nora's mother kissed Fake Nora's head and motioned for her to go down the hallway.

With her mother safely out of sight, Fake Nora turned abruptly and waved her fingers at Nora before dashing off. Nora watched anxiously as Fake Nora disappeared.

Nora turned on her heel and raced out of the room, heading down the hallway where her mother and her reflection had gone. She didn't see anything or anybody. And as she ran, there was still no sound of her feet. She knocked on her parents' door as she ran inside, knowing they'd be in there, and she could tell them the worst nightmare she'd ever had.

Like Nolan's, their bed was made, clean, dust-free, not lived in.

"What's happening?" Nora ran downstairs. Surely her family would be down there. It was probably a prank. It had to be a prank. "Very funny, guys! I get it. You've got me good. Now come out, okay?" She ran through the living room and kitchen. She raced through the study and the den.

Nothing.

No one.

No sound except for her own voice.

"Guys, please!" Her voice caught in her throat, and she felt like crying. This had to be a prank or a nightmare. It had to be something that would pass quickly. Either would be fine. Prank or Nightmare, it needed to be over soon.

When no sound came back to her, she raced to the door to look outside. She flung it open, expecting her family to be there, waiting for her.

Instead, she was met with darkness. Not darkness like nighttime, but darkness as in the color black, as in a void, as in nothing.

Like the house was the only thing in the world that existed.

She shut the door, locked it, and leaned her back on it. Her mind raced too quickly to form any kind of hypothesis of what was going on. It couldn't be a prank: not with the black void outside, and wouldn't she have woken up from a nightmare by now?

It didn't matter. Nightmare it was. She hurried up the steps to her room and slid under her comforter, covering her head and shutting her eyes tightly. Next to her sat her little stuffed animal, Hoppy, who was older than her and had helped her through many difficult situations. She hugged him to her chest, rocking back and forth under the covers.

Every possible scenario invaded her mind, from the plausible to the impossible. One impossible answer kept popping in her head, though. One she couldn't shake. One that could not be what happened, but seemed like the most likely of answers to her problem.

If she didn't know better—if she was a little child who believed in things like ghosts and magic, Nora would have thought that she had traded places with her reflection in the mirror. That the reflection, somehow, got out and was living her life while she was stuck in the world that existed only in mirrors, a boring world that she wanted out of as soon as possible.

But that couldn't happen, could it?

A person's reflection couldn't trade places with them.

Exhausted, Nora lay back against her soft pillows, kept her comforter over her head, hugged up to her favorite stuffed rabbit, Hoppy, and fell into a fitful sleep.

CHAPTER FIVE

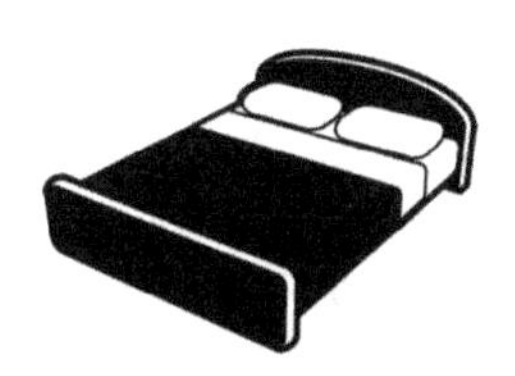

Nora rolled over and rubbed her eyes, trying to push the nightmare from the night before out of her mind. What a crazy nightmare it had been. She'd dreamed that a reflection had run away from her in that stupid old mirror in the guest room and that her parents and Nolan had disappeared. Oh, and there was no sound in the house except her. How weird was that?

Glad the nightmare was behind her, Nora sat up, gently laid Hoppy beside her, and stretched her tired muscles. No beams of sunshine shone through her window, which was strange, but not too strange. Yes, she normally got the morning sun in her room, but it probably meant that rain was on the way, which was fine with her. She liked rainy days as well as sunny ones, though sunny ones were more fun. Even if Nolan was seven years younger than her, she still took him outside on warm days and watched him as he played in his little kiddie pool. And sometimes, she'd get in the pool as well, just to watch her brother, of course. Not because she wanted to play in a kiddie pool. She was too old for them, but Nolan was just the right age. She did it for him, and only him.

That's what she told anyone who asked anyway.

Nora realized she must have woken up before everyone else in the house, strange for her. She thought she'd smell bacon and eggs cooking, like her mother normally cooked for her. She smelled nothing, literally nothing. No vanilla from her scented candle she got for Christmas last year. No spray her mother insisted she spray in the hallway for any kind of possible odors. No bacon. No eggs. No manly soap her dad used when he took a shower before work. The scent was normally so strong it wafted down the hallway and into Nora's room.

She smelled none of that. She smelled … nothing.

The scent matched the gray color coming from her window, which gave her a bit of a pause. Was her nose broken? Were her eyes playing tricks on her?

Nora knew Nolan was always up before her. He couldn't sleep past five-thirty to save his life. Needing to talk to him, Nora crawled out of her bed, and her feet hit the normally chilly floor. It wasn't cold at all. Not cold. Not hot. Nothing. No feeling at all, almost like the smells and the grayness.

Yup, she needed to get to Nolan fast. In her nightmare, he hadn't been in his bed. She needed to see him, to reassure herself that he was there, and he was okay. That everything was okay.

Pushing back all the strange feelings of the floor and all the other dull senses, Nora ran across the hallway into Nolan's room. She stopped inches from his bed when she realized it was made, and no one slept in it. In fact, she took a second to look around the room and, just as it had been last night in her nightmare, all his toys were perfectly placed where they were supposed to be. There was no mess, no clutter, no sign that an actual human lived there. It was a dull, lifeless perfection that made Nora's hair stand on end. She didn't like it. Not at all.

That had been a dream, right? A horrible nightmare, because what else could it have been?

"Mama?" Nora ran from Nolan's room, down

the hallway, and knocked on her parents' door. "Mama, are you awake?"

No answer.

"Daddy?" She pounded on the door harder, her heart starting to beat harder in her chest. "Daddy, are you there?"

No answer again.

She pounded harder to wake them up. They had to know Nolan was gone. They needed to look for him, bring him back. She never thought he'd run away, but he obviously had. What other explanation was there?

She pounded on the door again, harder, faster, more frantic. "Mama! Daddy, Nolan's gone!" Maybe if she told them about Nolan, then they'd be concerned enough to wake up. "Mama!"

Knowing she might get in trouble for opening the door and not caring, she turned the unlocked knob and opened the door. "Ma—" the word hung in her throat.

Inside her parents' room looked like Nolan's. Not exactly like Nolan's. His was a five-year-old boy's room. Her parents' room was painted a light purple with flowers hanging down from some of the walls. A nod to her mother's love of nature and all things natural. The bed with the lilac and white-colored comforter was perfectly made. No indents were on the bed covering to let her know that anyone had made it. It was as if the fabric simply lifted there and stayed naturally, or unnaturally. The same pale blue light that shined through her room had shown through her parents'.

It had been a dream, right?

Frantic—as she did in her nightmare—Nora ran down the stairs and searched for her parents and Nolan everywhere. Everywhere she looked was a dull impression of what the house usually looked like. The normally vibrant wall colors her mother loved so well were dulled, as if the house was awash in gray and sadness.

Nora remembered her nightmare from the night before. In that dream, she opened the front door and into a void of black. She refused to look out the door for fear it hadn't been a dream at all, as unlikely as that sounded. If she didn't look outside, she would never have to see if it was truly black outside, if it was exactly like her worst nightmare—literally.

Shaking, Nora went back up the stairs, holding onto the banister for support as she went up. In the dream, she remembered something about the mirror, the old mirror from the guest room. She'd looked in it and saw her reflection, only her reflection wasn't where it was supposed to be. Her reflection had been far away from her, at the door, and it had waved at her.

But that couldn't happen, right? It couldn't ...

Nora slowly crept back into the guest room with the gold walls and golden comforter on the bed. As the rest of the house, it seemed dulled, muted, and seemed to get grayer as the time went by, not that Nora knew what time it was. All the clocks were turned off. Even the old faithful grandfather clock downstairs hadn't struck in a while. Slowly, she crept toward the mirror on the dresser in the gold room. The closer she got, the colder the chill went up her spine. Instantly, she noticed it but tried to blink and pretend she hadn't seen it. If she didn't acknowledge it, then it wasn't real. If she didn't say it out loud or even think it, then it wasn't true.

Step by slow step, Nora inched toward the mirror, her gaze set straight in front of her, her body shaking as it tried to fight the truth, the realization of what was happening in front of her and what it potentially meant.

The closer she got to the mirror, nothing happened.

Sometimes, that's a good thing. Other times it isn't.

Normally, when one walks to a mirror, one is met with a reflection of themselves. Nora, however, wasn't as lucky. The door behind her was there. The edge of the bed filled the glass frame as did the gold curtains. The room looked exactly as it was supposed to in the reflection except for one thing.

Nora.

Nora's reflection was missing.

CHAPTER SIX

FAKE NORA

"Nora Elaine Williams, what has gotten into you?" Nora's mother bellowed from the kitchen. Nora … Fake Nora, though she felt very real, stood in the living room, hiding a laugh behind her hand.

"I don't know what you're talking about." She snickered, trying her best to hide the giggles inside. It wasn't working too well.

"The sink, Nora! You let the sink overflow, and there's water all over the floor."

"Oh, that. Yeah, whoops."

"Whoops!" She could almost hear Nora's mother's facial expression. She had to be irritated, furious even. Fake Nora tilted her head back and closed her eyes, drinking in the negative energy Nora's mother radiated. It tasted as sweet as the best candy, as delicious as the best cake ever created, as lovely as the most wonderful pie in the world. Fake Nora relished every single second of anger radiating off Nora's poor mother. It helped feed her soul, and her soul had been starving for quite some time, ever since they'd covered her mirror.

"You need to get in here and clean it up."

"I can't, Ma. I'm busy." Busy drinking in negative emotions, but that wasn't an important detail to tell her mother, now was it.

Fake Nora heard Nora's mother take a deep breath in the kitchen as if trying to calm her nerves. She had to give it to Nora's mother, she tried very hard to have a calm attitude. Fake Nora imagined she was one of those people who rarely got angry, and this was a rare occurrence for her. Fake Nora hated to tell her, but it would be a more normal occurrence now that she'd taken over Nora's life. Normally, she watched her reflections longer before taking over their lives, but it had been too long inside the mirror. And her hunger drew her out a lot sooner than normal, which was okay with her. Except it made acclimating to Nora's life a bit tricky. Though people rarely saw through the charade. She looked like Nora, talked like Nora, acted—about—

like Nora, and no one would ever suspect that she wasn't Nora.

She was something much older, much more dangerous, and much more evil, though she supposed evil was in the eye of the beholder.

Did hunger make her evil? No. Now, taking over people's lives to fill that hunger might, but that wasn't her fault, either. She couldn't help how she was born … made … she wasn't sure what she had been exactly.

"Nora, you made this mess, and it is your responsibility to clean it up. Leaving it isn't like you. You are normally more thoughtful than this."

Great, Fake Nora thought. It would be much more difficult to get full-on negative and angry emotions in a family that didn't have them very often. She'd have to fix that.

Until that time, she didn't want to raise any undue suspicions. She didn't want to be too unlike "Real Nora"—for now anyway. Later, when the family was destroyed, she didn't care what happened. She'd be fed. She'd have what she needed.

"Sorry, Ma. On my way." Fake Nora closed her eyes, drinking in the very last drop of anger radiating from her mother before it faded, and fade it did. Fake Nora, still hungry but not starving, wiped her mouth as if eating a delicious meal and took a deep breath. Yes, she'd bend to the family's rules for a while, but only for a while. She turned to go into the kitchen to clean up her mess, all the while whistling to herself and wondering if Real Nora had figured it out yet.

CHAPTER SEVEN

NORA

When there's no sound except the beating of your own heart in your ears, even the slightest sound can make you jump. The pebble hitting on a window somewhere in the house most certainly got Nora's attention. She wiped the tears that had fallen down her face as she stared at the void in the mirror. Nora ran through the house to find where the sound had come from. If there was a sound, that was good, right? It meant that she wasn't in some sort of horrible dream world where she was the only person around, and she'd never see her family again.

The thought of never seeing her mama, dad, or brother again made tears form in Nora's eyes. She'd been so terrified before that she hadn't thought about the implications of what she was going through. Would she be stuck ... wherever she was ... forever? Would there be a way to get away from there? Would she ever see her family?

Movement from her left caught her attention, and all thoughts of the pebble sound completely left her mind.

The movement came from the old antique mirror. And it was the reflection of her mother.

"Mama!" Nora ran to the mirror, beating at the glass for her mother to hear her. Her mother sighed as she ran her fingers over the old glass, not looking at Nora. Not seeing her.

Fear constricted Nora's heart as she beat on the mirror harder. She had to get her mama's attention. She had to get out of here! She'd hear her. She had to. Her mama would figure out a way to get her out. Nora had no doubts about that. "Mama, help me! I can't get out." She beat on the mirror so hard her hand stung. "Mama!"

Her mother put something down on the dresser under the mirror. Whatever it was, Nora couldn't see it. She did see her mama pulling her long red hair back into a ponytail. She also saw herself in the mirror, her reflection, the thing that wasn't her standing in the doorway of the room, like she didn't want to get close to the mirror. "I cleaned it, Ma."

"Thank you, Nora. Next time, just clean it to start with, alright?"

Fake Nora nodded before glaring into the mirror and sticking her tongue out at Nora.

"Did you see that?" Nora beat the glass, begging her mama to hear her. "That's not me! You know me! You know me!"

Fake Nora turned and bounced out of the doorframe as Nora's mother put the finishing touches on her hair. She pushed it up slightly on the sides and leaned her hands on the dresser.

"Everything okay?" Nora's dad came into the guest room in his Sunday clothes, black slacks and a blue button-up shirt.

"I don't understand Nora today." Her mother's shoulders slumped.

"That's because it's not me!" Nora yelled, tears stinging her eyes.

"Honey, she's just going through a phase. I hear they are normal for children her age." Her father hugged her mama from behind, and they both glanced at the mirror. Why couldn't they see her? What did she have to do to get their attention?

Surely, they wouldn't think that other Nora was her and claim her as their child forever, right? Right?

"I hope so. I miss my Nora. Do you know what she called me today? Ma."

"Oh, no. Let's call someone. That's horrible. She does need help." Her father chuckled, his face lighting up.

Her mother playfully elbowed him in the stomach. "I don't mean that. It's just, she's always called me Mama. Always. And I guess I'm not ready for her to grow up and not call me that."

"At least you still have Nolan." Her father kissed her ma gently on the temple.

"I'm right here!" Tears dripped down Nora's face and splashed on the dresser.

"I still have Nora, too," her mother said. "Okay, give me ten minutes, and I'll be ready for church."

"Deal." Her dad kissed her mama on the nose, and, hand in hand, they left the room.

Nora stopped beating the mirror. She stopped yelling for them to hear her. She watched, unable to blink or look away as her mama and daddy left her alone in that room, alone by herself, alone while they took care of some sort of … monster that wasn't her.

Nora's little dreary world folded in on her as she

fell to her knees in front of the mirror, never feeling more alone.

CHAPTER EIGHT

FAKE NORA

"Nora, why aren't you dressed yet?" Nora's mother came down the steps, placing an earring in her ear, looking at Fake Nora like she had done something wrong. In reality, Fake Nora had done something wrong, just not what Nora's mother thought she had.

"Is it Sunday?" Fake Nora hadn't thought about what day it was in a long time. She'd been stuck in that mirror for so long, she hadn't thought about days or weeks or months … or years since she could remember. She also couldn't remember what was so special about Sundays. It seemed like there was some thought, scratching at the back of her mind about Sundays and why they were special. But she couldn't pull it out of her mind, not that she thought too much about it. Nora's mother, she was sure, would tell her exactly what Sunday was.

"Has been all morning." Nora's mother laughed lightly. "Now run up to your room and put on a dress. We don't have much time."

Fake Nora stood, not wanting to leave the house so early. She hadn't gotten acclimated to the surroundings yet. She hadn't gotten to know her family that well, the life she'd taken over. She'd been stuck in that glass for no telling how long and things, it seemed, had changed. There were things on the wall she had no idea about. A large rectangular box with moving pictures sat not far from her. And everything was simply strange. She'd picked up Nora's cadence as she spoke the few minutes she'd heard her with the drape pulled over the glass. Such a smart family, the last family she inhabited was. She had no doubts Nora's people weren't nearly as bright, not as bright to lock her away in a mirror.

No, she would be Nora from now until she decided it wouldn't be a good fit for her anymore, and honestly, Fake Nora thought that would be a long time away.

"I'm ... not feeling myself today." She told Nora's mother as she stood and held her stomach. It wasn't the least bit a lie. Fake Nora did not, in fact, feel herself.

"I noticed that this morning." Nora's mother came over and pressed her hand to Fake Nora's forehead. Fake Nora flinched at the contact. No one had touched her so tenderly in so long. Probably since her own mother from so far away, Fake Nora couldn't recall how long ago it had been. The other families she'd inhabited, all were mostly not kind to each other, which made scaring them and eating their fear that much more enjoyable. And Fake Nora did enjoy the taste of Nora's mother's fear. It had tasted so good this morning, and she couldn't wait to get more of it later.

But for now, she enjoyed pretending that she was actually Nora, and her mother was actually caring for her. She'd missed contact being stuck in that mirror so long by herself.

"No fever." Nora's mother said, rubbing Fake Nora's head once more. "Does your stomach hurt?"

Fake Nora nodded. She'd have said anything hurt to stop from leaving the house.

"What about church? The youth were going to a performance today. You'll miss out."

Church ... Fake Nora nearly choked at the word. That's what she knew happened on Sunday, and that's someplace she didn't want to go. Church burned her skin, from the inside, of course. It didn't hurt the reflection she inhabited, but, inside, it hurt. It burned. It felt like she wanted to be in the building, but she didn't belong. Fake Nora recalled a far, far away memory of being in a church when she was all too human. She remembered liking it, the hymns. The pretty dresses. The statues. The beautiful pictures hanging on the wall.

She shook her head, pushing those long-ago memories away. There was no reason to think about them. She'd never be able to go back to those simpler times. Her own mother had made certain of that.

"I know I'll miss it, and I'm sorry. I just don't feel well today. I think I need to lie down." Fake Nora ran by Nora's mother without stopping for any answer. She ran past Nora's father on the steps and into Nora's room. She plopped down on the bed and plastered her face in the pillow. The bed felt wonderful against her weary bones. Her body took the physical form of whatever reflection she chose, or whatever reflection she had to choose, but her soul—her real self was ancient. Much older to count, and her bones felt it. Sometimes she wished hopping from reflection to reflection made you young again. Relive times gone by and mistakes you could change.

"Nora, are you not coming to church?" Nolan, Nora's little brother, asked from the doorway. He was a little thing, probably five or six. Cute as a button. Fake Nora just wanted to eat him up. She put aside all thoughts of the past and focused on the here and now, just as she always did. And here and now, there was a little child who was ripe for the picking. Adult fear tasted sweet. Child fear tasted like a marvelous feast.

"Not today." Fake Nora smiled at the child and made sure her mouth contorted in an ever so eerie grin, one that wasn't noticeable to others, but one that caused uneasiness in the person she showed it to. That person was her new favorite target, Nora's little brother.

Oh, she smiled as Nora's brother's eyes got big before he ran down the hallway. The fear that radiated off him gave her a lovely snack, and she laid her head down on the pillow satisfied.

She only had to fool the parents ... not the kid. The kid she could do whatever she wanted to. They wouldn't believe him anyway.

Fake Nora laid on her back and smiled at the ceiling. She pushed down all the nervousness that always filled her when she traded places with another reflection and sucked in a deep breath. This wasn't a bad place. Not bad at all. And way better than the mirror.

She smiled at the ceiling. She wondered how ole Nora was doing in Reflectionland. She wondered if she'd met her fellow prisoners yet.

CHAPTER NINE

NORA

Another pebble sound filled the room, catching Nora's attention. She had no idea how long she'd been crying, but she knew that she most certainly hadn't been the one to throw a stone or pebble or whatever. She also knew that whatever was happening was actually happening. It wasn't a dream or a tale. It wasn't anything as simple as that. She was really in that place, behind the mirror, wherever it was, and she had to find some way out of it.

Standing, Nora decided she had one thing she needed to do first. It hurt too much to see her parents going on with their life like she was there, because, to them, she *was* there. But to her, she knew she wasn't. So, as much as it hurt her to do it, she grabbed the golden comforter from the bed and tossed it over the mirror, not wanting to see her real house if she couldn't be in it herself.

With the mirror covered, the dim house almost felt like hers. She could imagine her parents and little brother were simply outside playing and would come in when it got dark.

Nora had a great imagination. During classes she didn't particularly like at school, she daydreamed, thinking about incredibly elaborate stories and places she'd love to visit. No one ever caught her either, which had been a plus.

Another pebble sound filled the room. It was a strange sound, not an echo in the least. Nothing in this house echoed. But it filled the room nonetheless. She knew it was coming from somewhere close to her, but she couldn't place where.

Determined to find the culprit, Nora left the guest room, closing the door shut behind her. Upon inspecting the floor in the hallway, Nora discovered there were no pebbles or stones anywhere. There wasn't anything on the floor at all. Nothing to cause that noise that she knew for certain she had heard.

Or had she?

Her mind had played tricks on her before in this place, hadn't it? What if she had heard something that was happening on the other side of the mirror —as strange as that was to think—and she only thought it was really happening to her in her reflection world?

Nora became very still. There wasn't any sound, which made the seconds move by agonizingly slow. She didn't hear her breath at all or any sound that resembled a pebble. Her heart dropped when she realized that she must have only heard something happening in her real life, through the mirror. Now that it was covered, she wouldn't hear it. It made her want to go and uncover it, and she turned to do just that.

Another sound of a pebble came from downstairs.

Nora couldn't be sure it was a pebble, of course. It could be anything. What it sounded like was something hard hitting something solid like metal or glass. It reminded her of a pebble she used to throw at a tin rooster on her grandfather's farm when she was little, which is why, she assumed, she thought of it as a pebble. Though she supposed it could be anything.

This pebble sound came from downstairs. This was different than it was before, right?

Another pebble sound came from downstairs, making Nora jump. Whatever it was, was it trying to get her attention? She couldn't be sure. She also couldn't be sure it was a good idea to go and investigate it. Once in her life, she'd seen a scary movie. Her parents had watched one a few years ago, thinking she and Nolan were already in bed. Nolan had been asleep. Nora had specifically not, just so she could sneak and sit in the crack of their doorway and watch the movie that they had on in their room. Due to the scariness of the monster, the blood, and the jumpscares, she'd lasted all of fifteen minutes. A respectable time, she thought. Basically, Nora wasn't a very brave person. She knew it. She accepted it.

But now she felt like she needed to be brave. She wanted to go downstairs and investigate the sound. She needed to. If it got her out of this place, she didn't think she had any choice.

Then again, what if it was something worse than her evil reflection? What if there were things in the house, bad things, that wanted to eat real people like her? What if something waited for her downstairs like she was a good feast, and her parents would never know that she was ever missing, and her reflection would take over her life forever?

Her stomach began aching so bad, and she felt sick. She ran to the bathroom, shut the door behind her, and locked it. No real person-eating monster was going to gobble her up. Not today. She crawled over to the toilet and tossed up the lid, just in case she really did throw up.

"You won't get me here," she whispered to the monsters downstairs, now that she was locked safely in a room where nothing would ever get her.

"You sound so sure of that."

Nora jumped and backed away from the toilet and didn't stop until her back hit the wall behind her so hard it nearly knocked the wind out of her. She rubbed her aching back, looking around frantically so she could see what had talked to her.

Not seeing anything, Nora grabbed a bottle of her shampoo from the tub and held it out in front of her like a weapon. "Who are you? What are you doing inside my house?"

She looked all around: up on the towel shelves, in the linen closet, under the sink. Everywhere and nowhere held the culprit.

"Who are you?" she yelled, holding her shampoo out with trembling fingers.

"You really think you are going to hurt me with that" The voice was male, probably around her age if she had to guess. But where was he? She turned, thinking he might sneak up behind her like a shadow.

"I can try." She gritted her teeth, hoping she sounded incredibly scary and intimidating.

"You can do that, but I do believe it would take much more than that." He seemed to be laughing at her. Where was he?

Nora glanced around the room once more, and, finally, her eyes landed on the mirror above the sink. In it stood a boy around her age with floppy dirty blond hair and overalls. Instead of the bathroom as one would expect to see in a reflection of a bathroom, Nora saw the boy stood in a living room of some type. Old, certainly, but it didn't appear old. It looked as if one of those old pictures she'd seen at her grandfather's farm had turned into color, and everything was new and fresh, only from a long-forgotten era.

The walls behind the boy were a creamy white color, a wooden sofa with dark red fabric sat right behind him. There were two rocking chairs on each side. If Nora thought of the mirror as a painting, to the right of the boy was a door that led into what appeared to be a kitchen with some sort of … stove … maybe. If it was a stove, it wasn't like anything she'd seen before. The contraption was bulky, black, and looked like it would burn anything that touched it. She wouldn't want anything like that around Nolan. He'd burn his fingers off. How did the boy or his family not burn their fingers?

To his right was an entryway to what looked like a foyer and then maybe stairs leading to a second floor. Nora couldn't be sure of that.

He dropped something from his hand, which landed on the floor in a thud. Nora recognized the sound. It was the pebbles from before. But if he threw them, then how did the sound get downstairs?

"You appear confused." He crossed his arms and stared up at her. The way he stood made Nora think the mirror he looked in hung high on a wall, perhaps over a fireplace or something.

"I'm sure I do, since I am confused." Nora slid down to the floor, her legs unable to hold her up any longer. She sat the shampoo bottle on the floor next to her in case she needed to grab it quickly. It's not like she knew what was going on or the rules of the house. For all she knew, the boy could leap out of the mirror and attack her. Thinking that, she moved the shampoo bottle closer to her side, hoping he didn't see her.

"My name is Jesse. Jesse Sanford. And you are?"

"Nora Williams." It felt so surreal to be having this conversation with someone in a mirror, someone who shouldn't be in her house, in her bathroom, or behind the glass.

"I'm thirteen. How old are you?"

An older boy. Nora blushed slightly before she realized that there was no reason to blush. None of this made any sense anyway. "Twelve."

His face fell slightly like all those older boys at schools did when they found out she was younger than them. "But I'll be thirteen in ten months."

"Ah." He ran his fingers through his disheveled hair. "Where are you?"

"In my house."

"No, where are you place-wise?"

"Oh, uh, Tennessee."

Jesse's eyes narrowed. "Where at in Tennessee?"

"Cross Plains. Why?"

Jesse scoffed and shook his head while looking at the ground. "Nothing. It's not important."

Nora figured everything was important, but she let his unusual reaction go. "How can you see me?"

"Same as you, I imagine, looking through a mirror. I'm in my living room, but I can't place where you are."

Nora looked around. Seemed pretty typical of a room to her. "Bathroom. Restroom, I guess you could call it."

"Bathroom? Geez, you must be rich to have an outhouse in your house."

"An outhouse? No … what … no, it's what everyone has."

"I don't. And I've only ever heard of rich people having indoor plumbing. Man, I bet he's enjoying it there."

"One, everyone has indoor plumbing. Some people even have two or three bathrooms."

"No kidding?"

"No kidding."

"Huh …" he said thoughtfully. "What year is it where you are?"

His question threw her off guard. What did he mean, what year was it? It was the same year it was everywhere.

When she told him the answer, his eyes grew wide as saucers. His skin paled as if he might pass out right then and there. "Why? What year did you think it was?"

"I thought ... I thought it was the year it is."

"Then ... why did you act so strangely?"

He shook his head. "No. You misunderstand me. I mean, I thought it was the year it is where I am."

"What year is it where you are?" A sentence Nora never thought she'd say.

"Nineteen hundred forty."

Nora sat up straighter. "Excuse me? You're in the past?"

"No, you're in the future."

"No ... I'm not. That's the present year. It's currently the *now* year. Your year is the past. Like eighty years in the past."

Jesse staggered back a bit and sat down gingerly on the coffee table. "I knew it felt like I'd been stuck here forever. I never imagined I really had."

"Where are we stuck? What's happened to us?" Nora didn't know if she wanted to know. Yes, she did, and no, she didn't. If she didn't know, she could imagine it would all be okay. She'd go to bed, cover her head, and stay there until things got right with the world again. Or she could imagine her family outside playing, and they'd come in soon. Like she thought before, Nora had a great imagination and could come up with all sorts of stories to tell herself so she wouldn't be so scared.

But they would be just that, stories. They wouldn't mean anything, and they wouldn't be true. They most certainly wouldn't get her out of the dim house and back to her family.

"Have you seen him?" Jesse asked curiously.

"Seen who? I've not seen anybody here except me."

He shook his head. "No, not where you are. Not in the house you are in, with your rich bathrooms, but in the mirror."

"I see you in my mirror."

"No." He grumbled. "No. The other mirror. The one that's attached to an old dresser. My pa bought it for my ma. The first new bit of furniture she'd ever owned, even if it was used. She picked it out and everything. She loved it at first sight. She put it in her room, and I swear, I just went in to take a peek. One quick peek. Then I saw myself in the reflection, only it wasn't me. It was me, but it wasn't. Do you understand?"

Nora understood, and it made her skin chill. "It was your reflection, but it wasn't acting like a reflection. It wasn't following you around."

"At first, it was. Then, it just stopped. I felt this

tingle start at my toes then go up my legs. It was like I was drawn to the mirror. I had to touch it. I had to. And then … then I was all alone and he, Fake me, had my life."

Nora's stomach churned. "Same thing happened to me, only it was a girl, 'cause she looked like me. And I woke up here. Alone until I heard you. Are there others? I heard sounds from downstairs."

"No!" Jesse stood up quickly and raced toward the mirror, causing Nora to jump backward, hitting her new bruise again on the wall. She wished pain was like sound here, dull. "No, don't go to any other mirror except this one and the one you disappeared from. Don't answer any more calls or voices. Trust me."

Nora didn't know why she should trust him when she'd only met him. And hadn't he called her to come to see him, too?

"I'm serious, Nora. There are things in the other mirrors … in the house. They'll get you, if you let them. They'll trick you, and you won't know who to trust. You're new to this. I'm not. I know what I'm talking about."

"How do I know I can trust you?" She wanted more than anything to trust him, but how was she supposed to know? He'd done the exact same thing he'd said not to trust. That didn't exactly cause trust.

"You don't," he answered simply. "But you definitely can't trust them."

"Who's them?"

"Bad ones, Nora. Bad ones."

CHAPTER TEN

FAKE NORA

Fake Nora laid on Nora's bed, staring at her ceiling for a while, not sure what she wanted to do with her afternoon. She could check on Nora, of course. Look in the mirror and see what she was into. She wondered if she'd met the bad ones yet. If she had, well, Fake Nora didn't miss them at all.

Sounds. She'd forgotten about sounds and how things in the real world echoed, how alive they felt. Not like how they felt in the mirror. Everything there was dead, gray, decaying. It had no life to it. The real world had life. It had sounds. Fake Nora had missed sounds so much!

The sound she found most appealing was the grandfather clock ticking away downstairs. In one of her habitats, the family had two grandfather clocks, and no matter what the father did, the clocks never ticked at the same time, so it was a continuous tick-tick … tick-tick … and at the time, it had annoyed Fake Nora to no end. She'd ended up covering the family's noses with pillows one night, drinking in all the fear, which was delicious to the last drop before she found another family to drain dry.

The grandfather clock downstairs struck twelve, and Fake Nora heard footsteps coming up to her room. A few seconds later, she was met with the worst smell she'd ever smelled in her life: human food.

"Nora, I brought you some chicken noodle soup." Nora's mother stood in the doorway of the room, holding a tray with steaming hot soup that burned Fake Nora's nose and made her want to throw up. She tried to remember a time when she ate human food, probably when she was human, but now the mere thought of it made her sick. Human food was the one thing she hated about being in the real world. She much preferred fear.

Fear made the world go round.

Fear tasted delicious.

Human food was worse than dirt.

"Thanks, Ma." Fake Nora sat up and tried to

hide her revulsion as Nora's mother put the tray in her lap.

Nora's mom felt her head again.

"I'm feeling much better," Fake Nora said, turning the disgusting soup over in her spoon.

She was very careful not to look at her reflection in the metal. Looking at her reflection would be disastrous.

"Good. I'm glad." Nora's mother patted Fake Nora on the head and started out the door. "Honey, I was wondering, what has gotten into you?"

Fake Nora tried to remain calm. Humans never believed in the supernatural. Nora's mother was no exception. She would be just like all the families before and know that she was who she said she was, except for the Sanford family. They had figured it out, and it had cost her years in that blasted mirror.

No matter. She'd spent her time learning and working on ways to improve her mimicking techniques. She wouldn't be placed in another mirror this time.

"What do you mean?" Fake Nora picked up a piece of toast and bit the tiniest piece off the edge to show Nora's mother that she was completely fine. The burned bread tasted like muck in her mouth, and it took everything Fake Nora had in her not to spit it out. It sure wouldn't help her cause any.

"I mean, like this morning in the kitchen. You left a mess and didn't clean it up."

Fake Nora knew she should have waited a few hours before turning on the evil, scary Nora act. But she'd been starving, and desperate times called for desperate measures. She couldn't say she regretted it, only that she regretted Nora's mother being suspicious so soon.

"I told you, I was sorry about that," Fake Nora said in her best sincere voice.

"I know, and I do accept it. But there's something else, too. You started calling me Ma today."

Fake Nora hesitated a bit. The last reflection, Jesse, had called his parents Ma and Pa. Had she been in that mirror so long that people didn't do that anymore? Did they call them something else she didn't know about? Did they call them by their first names? That seemed highly unlikely, but what did she know about how life was in the future? "Just trying out something new to see if I like it."

Nora's mom frowned slightly.

"And you ... to see if you liked it ... I mean, I can change it back to ..." What had she called her before? "Um ... I can call you whatever you want if it would make you feel better. I don't want to upset you." Not now, Fake Nora thought with a sly, little inward laugh.

"No, it's fine," Nora's mother said with her own smile. "I get it that you are growing up, and you don't want to be defined by any sort of childish thing. I do admit that I thought you'd call me Mom before Ma, which is an interesting choice, by the way, but it's fine. I have to let you grow up sometime." Nora's mother pulled Fake Nora into a hug, which Fake Nora tried very hard not to pull away from. She couldn't remember the last time she'd had a hug, and, truthfully, she didn't much care for it. Hugs were restricting. She couldn't run if she needed to run. They got her too close to the parents, who might find out she wasn't the real Nora, even though she didn't think that would happen. This mom seemed like the kind of person who would believe anything of her child. She seemed to want to believe anything Nora said in the interest of her growing up, not like Jesse's parents, who saw through everything quickly and sent Fake Nora … Fake Jesse at the time … away.

"I can call you Mama still. It doesn't bother me." Fake Nora pushed back as easily as she could, which was difficult since Fake Nora was strong, part of her curse—or her blessing—depended on the day.

"I mean, if you want. I'll answer to it." Nora's mother kissed Fake Nora on the head and released her from the hug. Fake Nora breathed in some fresh, non-constricted air. Finally!

"If you are feeling better, I was going to cook some chicken and dumplings for lunch to eat when the boys get home. If you want ..."

Yuck. "Sounds good ... Mama." Fake Nora tried the word out on her lips. It felt strange, but it worked, and if it kept her in Nora's mother's good graces, then it would work. The only person she needed to feed off—for now—was the little brother. He'd feed her well, and she wouldn't have to worry about the parents for a long while, at least until she came up with a plan for what she would do next, where she'd go.

First, she'd need to figure out how old everyone had to be for different situations in life. Names for parents had changed. Fake Nora wondered what else had changed. Did the ages for getting a job change since Jesse's time? So she could live on her own and not be forced to go back into a mirror and change her reflection? She could, of course. She could go in any mirror she wanted at any time, but, as she'd learned, that left a bit of a problem. It made her vulnerable to be trapped in there, something she didn't want to happen anymore.

Nora's mom smiled down at Fake Nora. "Good. I'm glad you are feeling better, and I'm glad we got to talk."

"Me, too." Fake Nora forced her lips to curl into a smile. She hoped it wasn't too frightening. That had been her mistake at Jesse's house. She'd come on too strong too quickly. She didn't want to do that now. She'd learned from her mistakes.

Nora's mother left, and Fake Nora sat back down on the bed. She put the bowl of soup as far away from herself as possible, but it didn't take the horrible smell away. The smell felt like it was burning her nose. Ick.

Fake Nora got up and found an indoor outhouse, which was kind of interesting, to be honest. She was glad she hadn't been caught looking for an outhouse outside. Nora's ma would have definitely looked at her strangely then. Fake Nora brushed her teeth and did everything she needed to do in the bathroom without looking at the mirror. No mirrors. No reflections. That was the only way to keep her safely in the real world.

Fake Nora knew one thing for certain: under no

circumstance would she go back to Reflection World where everything was cold, dim, dreary. Nothing had a taste or smell. There was no real fear to feed on, and she nearly starved.

Here, she had it made. What luck that Nora had a little brother! Everything was working out perfectly for Fake Nora. Finally, after all these years, she was getting what she wanted, what she deserved.

All she had to do was keep Nora's little brother terrified, and everything would work out great.

The front door slammed downstairs, and the voices of Nora's father and brother echoed up the stairs into the bathroom. Speak of the devil, Nora's brother was home.

Time for lunch.

CHAPTER ELEVEN

NORA

"Bad ones?" Nora shuddered at the words. "Who are the bad ones?"

Jesse got very close to the mirror, which seemed to be difficult since his mirror was hung high on a wall, and he wasn't tall enough to get too close. "The bad ones are how they sound. Bad."

"What do they look like?" Chills ran all up and down Nora's arms. She didn't like the idea of being stuck here in the place anyway. Being stuck here with so-called "bad ones" didn't make her feel any better.

"I don't know. I've never seen them."

Nora scoffed. "Then how do you know they are bad? They could be trapped here like you, like us. They could need help."

Jesse shook his head vehemently with each word Nora spoke. “It’s not like that. The bad ones, I hear them. They howl and scratch. They pretend they are human, but they aren’t. Sometimes, I hear them talking, and they say the most horrible things.”

“If they aren’t human, how can they talk?” ’Cause that seemed a logical question to her.

“Maybe they were human at one time, but they aren’t anymore. I think they are real people who were turned into reflections like us only a long, long time ago. I think they’ve been stuck here so long that they aren’t human anymore, and they do bad things.”

Nora swallowed hard. “Do you think that’ll happen to us?”

Jesse didn’t answer with words, but he looked away from the mirror, which terrified Nora.

“I don’t want to be a bad one.” Nora’s voice quivered.

“I don’t either,” Jesse answered sadly, clutching his fist at his side. “I think, though, if you are stuck here long enough, it is inevitable.”

“Then … then we find a way out. There has to be a way. I mean, the reflection left, right? Doesn’t that mean that there is a way for us to leave?”

“I’ve tried everything I can think of,” Jesse

admitted. "I don't have any ideas, but if you do, I'm all ears."

A low rumbling started from the bottom floor and radiated up the stairs, which shocked Nora since there were no echoes where she was. Jesse turned around behind him like he heard a noise where he was, too. When he faced his mirror again, his eyes were huge. "That's the bad ones. Don't go toward them, okay, Nora? Don't."

"But they can help." Nora had hope they could, at least. Hope that she wasn't alone and someone could help her.

"No!" He practically jumped at the mirror. "No, don't. I promise you, they aren't any good."

"But you said you haven't seen them," she reminded him.

Jesse bit his bottom lip like he didn't know if he should say anything or not.

"Jesse, you can't keep things in here from me. I need to know what's going on so I can get out of here." She thought the word maybe … *maybe* get out of here, but she wouldn't let her mouth say it. She would get out of that place and back home. She would. It was only a matter of time. And if Jesse knew something that would help her, then she needed to know.

"You weren't the first girl I've talked to here, you know," Jesse began. He sounded so sad. "There was another who was here when I got here. Her name was Martha. Martha was twenty, I think. She was married with a daughter when she was taken. She watched as that thing, that reflection, took over her life, took over her family, scared them to death … and it turned Martha. It turned her into a bad one. One day she just, snapped. It was instant, though I assume it had taken many years to do so. It was … it was bad."

"Have you seen her since?"

He shook his head. "That's the thing with the bad ones. You don't see them. They like, lose their reflection. They become invisible. Ghosts of themselves. Ghosts in a reflection-world, which I imagine is a horrible thing. They lose themselves. They lose everything." Jesse lowered his head and shut his eyes. "I don't want to turn into one of them."

Nora didn't want him to turn into one of them, either. She didn't want to turn into one of them. "I suppose when you turn into a bad one, you can't go back home."

Jesse smiled sadly. "I don't think you can go back home anyway, but when you turn into a bad one, there's nothing to go back home to. No person anyway. You become this thing. This ghost." Jesse visibly shuddered. "I'm not sure what happens after that. Except there is a lot of screams, and they attack. I don't want to be one of the things that attacks you."

"You won't." Nora had never felt so sure of anything in her life. "We'll get out of here, Jesse. I promise you. We will."

"You're new. You have no idea what this place is. Do you think I've just been sitting in this room forever? Just twiddling my thumbs and not doing anything to get out, to get home? I have, Nora. I've tried. And it's impossible. I'm sorry, but it is."

She shook her head. "No. I don't believe that. There has to be a way. There has to be a way to do it."

"I wish you were right. I wish so much you were right, but there isn't. There just isn't. And if the place doesn't get you, if you don't turn into a bad one, you'll be haunted by them. They'll never let you rest, never let you sleep, never leave you alone. It gets worse, Nora. The experience here gets so much worse. If you think this is bad, you have no idea. None. I'm sorry, Nora, but you are stuck, and the quicker you get that through your mind and learn how to dodge the bad ones, the better off you'll be. Do you understand me?"

Nora crossed her arms defiantly. "I don't. I don't understand. How could you just give up?"

Jesse turned his back to the mirror. "Gah, you are impossible. Impossible! Fine, you do whatever you think you have to do to get out of here. Go ahead, but don't come crying to me when the bad ones get you, or when you start to turn into one of them yourself, because it will happen, Nora. It'll happen, and you won't be ready for it because you've spent your time believing in fairy tales. That you thought there was a way out."

Nora refused to let the tears threatening to fall, fall. Jesse didn't know everything. He might think he did, but he didn't. If she was determined to do anything, it happened. She was determined to get out of here, to get home. Her parents missed her. She had no doubt that they'd realized Fake Nora wasn't here. They were probably on the other side, trying to figure out how to get her home. And if Jesse thought she was going to sit here and do nothing, then he was mistaken. She couldn't let her parents down, who she was sure were worried to death about her.

Determined, she stood and placed the shampoo

bottle back in the shower. "Guess this is good-bye then."

Jesse turned back to her, fear in his eyes. "What does that mean? You don't want to talk to me anymore?"

She didn't want to tell him, but he was a bit depressing to talk to. He was very negative, and negativity wasn't anything that could help her. She needed focus. She needed a way back to her parents, and she didn't see Jesse helping her. "I don't mind talking to you, but you said you didn't want to see me when I failed, and I don't intend on failing. I am getting out of here, Jesse. You can believe me or not. It doesn't matter to me, but what does matter is that I'm going to get out of here. You can either come with me or not. It's up to you, but I'm not giving up. If you want me to talk to you again, then you don't need to give up, either."

He smirked and shook his head. "You are a determined one, I'll give you that."

"My parents miss me."

"They don't know you're gone, sweetheart."

Ah! "Don't sweetheart me … sweetheart. They do know I'm gone. And if you don't want to help me, that's fine. I'll do it myself. Nice talking to you.

See you … never." In a huff, Nora opened the bathroom door.

"Don't say I didn't warn you," Jesse said before Nora shut the door on him. She leaned back against the wall, irritated as all get out. How could he be so cold? How could he not want to get out of here? How could he deter her if she wanted to find a way out? Just because he hadn't didn't mean she wouldn't.

Nora took a deep breath, determined to find some way back home. As she stood in the dim, quiet hallway, her conviction started to go away. Out here, the reality of where she was and the task at hand hit her hard. Out here, she knew the bad ones might pop up at any time. Out here, she had to be on her guard.

Part of her wanted to run back to Jesse and stay in the bathroom with the door locked forever. Another part of her knew she couldn't do that. Just because she had no idea how to get home didn't mean there wasn't a way. She just had to find it.

She prayed, Lord, please let me find it.

CHAPTER TWELVE

FAKE NORA

Fake Nora made it through lunch.

She even ate some of the regretful chicken and dumplings. They turned her stomach and made her sick with every bite, but she'd done it. It wasn't that she couldn't eat human food. She absolutely could. Wasn't her favorite, though.

The good part of the meal came from Nora's little brother, Nolan, who apparently hadn't forgotten her overly exaggerated smile earlier. She smelled the fear on him all through lunch, and oh how lovely it tasted. Nora covered each bite of human food by drinking the fear radiating off of Nolan, and it was wonderful. Wonderful.

"The preacher said to tell you she missed you at

church today," Nora's dad said, grabbing another helping of dumplings.

"Thanks. I just wasn't feeling myself." She pointedly looked at Nora's little brother, who she thought would choke on his chicken. "I'm feeling much better now, Daddy."

Fake Nora noticed that Nora's little brother stopped chewing when she said that. Perhaps, he was hoping his big sister was back for good. Maybe he thought what he'd seen earlier was a fluke, a trick of the light. Surely, his big sister couldn't be some sort of weird monster. That would be insane, right?

Good, she'd give him a little reprieve. Fear tasted much better in waves, and she had plenty of time. Fake Nora had no intention of leaving this family anytime soon, though in a few weeks, days even, Nora's little brother would probably wish she would leave.

After lunch, the family went their separate ways. Nora's mom and dad went to their room to watch a movie. Nora's little brother went up to his room to play with his toys, and Fake Nora went through the house, looking around, glancing at pictures on strange appliances to get accustomed to this family, this time period, these people. She didn't want any more mess-ups like she'd had with Ma and Mama. Such a silly little mistake that had truly thrown Nora's mother for a curve. This family wasn't like Jesse's, which Fake Nora appreciated.

Once Fake Nora was finished looking at everything downstairs and locking it securely in her memory, she began wondering how Nora was. Now, it was a gamble to look in the mirror she came out of, any reflection, really, was a gamble. But she could chance it every so often for a few seconds. No doubt, Nora hadn't figured out how to send her back to the reflection world yet ... and she never would. So checking in on her little friend, for a few seconds, wouldn't be bad.

Fake Nora bounced up the stairs. Why did she have to be quiet now? The bad ones weren't around in this world. They couldn't kill Fake Nora, but they could annoy her. They couldn't annoy her here, which Fake Nora loved. No little bad ones gnats flying around. It made for an enjoyable afternoon.

When she got to the guest room with the golden walls, Fake Nora walked over to the mirror, not looking at the reflection just yet. She'd only glance at it, give herself a second or two, then look away. Life was nothing but a gamble, right?

Any human looking in the mirror would see a reflection of Nora. Fake Nora, though, saw what was really there, and laughed. Nora had placed something over the mirror, a comforter, maybe? A blanket? Fake Nora laughed some more. Why had Nora done that? Did she think it would keep her from going back? Did she actually want to stay in Reflection World? Fake Nora didn't understand it, and she looked away with tears in her eyes from laughing so hard.

"What's so funny?" Nolan asked from the doorway, a little truck held in each hand.

She dried her tears and decided it was time for a snack. "Just the mirror. I think it's haunted."

"Haunted? Like with ghosts?" His little child eyes widened.

"Like with ghosts. And I think if you look in it, you'll see them."

Nora's brother shook his head and backed away. "I don't want to see ghosts."

"Scared?" She knew he was. She smelled the sweet scent on him. She loved it.

"No." He stood straighter, slightly trembling. "I'm five. I don't get scared."

"Okay." Fake Nora tried not to giggle. This little feller was going to be so much fun. "Go back and play with your toys. Just remember, don't look in the mirrors. The ghosts will get you."

"You're making up stories," he said with his five-year-old brevity.

"I'm not."

"You are. I'm telling Mama."

"Go ahead. She won't believe you. She'll think you're making it up." Fake Nora got very close to Nora's brother, leaning down until she was inches from his face. She made sure to put that smile on her face that had scared him earlier, just for effect. "She'll believe me over you any day."

Nora's brother ran from the room and slammed his door. Fake Nora followed behind, drinking in all the fear he'd left behind like a Hansel and Gretel trail. Oh yes, Nora's brother would be a great many feasts.

CHAPTER THIRTEEN

NORA

Once Nora was outside of the bathroom, all of her brevity slid away. She wanted to run back and tell Jesse she was sorry, and she'd never leave the confines of the room again. Not ever. She'd die in there if she had to. No, she wouldn't die. According to Jesse, she would disappear and turn into a ghost of a reflection: a bad one.

That sounded horribly not great.

From what she had gathered, and wished she'd asked Jesse more questions about before heading out into the unknown, the bad ones were free to wander around the houses as they pleased. They didn't have to have mirrors to connect with people like she and Jesse seemed to need. So that was nice.

Not only did Nora need to figure out how to get

back to her parents, she needed to figure out how to keep away from the bad ones and not become a bad one herself.

She could do this.

She could.

She had faith in herself that this would be okay.

She'd find a way out. She was sure Jesse or Martha hadn't tried all the options. They probably gave up way before she did. Nora wouldn't give up. She wasn't a quitter, and that would be how she got out of the house when they couldn't. There wasn't a rule book to this, and if for some reason someone actually had written a rule book for it, Nora would throw it out the window. Thanks to the prayer that went up earlier and her own wonderful new pep talk, Nora felt confident again. Confident and wishing she had some sort of weapon against the bad ones.

Remembering something, Nora ran to Nolan's room and grabbed his little plastic bat from beside his bed. The little blue bat felt flimsy in her hand, like it wouldn't hurt anything, and it most certainly wouldn't scare anything. But, it made her feel protected and like David going after Goliath, she headed out to find a way out of the house, bat in hand.

The no echo thing hurt her ears once more, and she decided she didn't have to live in silence. "This little light of mine ... I'm gonna let it shine." She barely sang above a whisper.

That actually helped a little bit.

She crept down the hallway toward the stairs, choking the bat for dear life.

"This ... little light ... of mine ..."

Step.

Step.

"I'm gonna let it shine ..."

Step.

Closer to the steps.

"This ... little light of mine ..."

Step.

Then she was right on the top step, peering down the stairs to the front door. If this place was anything like the dream that wasn't a dream, the front door would be black behind it. That could be a way out, and she didn't want to not try it as an escape simply because she was afraid. Being afraid wouldn't get her back home. No, that wasn't right: acting in fear wouldn't get her back home. She could be afraid all she wanted, and it was okay to be afraid. But she couldn't let that fear keep her in that house like it did Jesse and Martha. She refused to turn into a bad one.

"I'm … gonna …"

Step.

"Let … it shine."

Step.

Step.

Choking the bat.

The door was right there.

Right in front of her.

"Let it shine. Let it shine …"

Step.

Step.

"Let … it …"

Every door downstairs slammed, making Nora jump, drop her bat, and run back up the stairs. Gusts of wind followed her, hurricane gusts of wind that made her hair fly around her face in all directions. She grabbed the banister of the stairs and pulled, dragging herself to the second-floor landing. The downstairs sounded like an explosion, doors slamming over and over and over, mixed with the no echoes around her.

She ran to the bathroom door, locked it behind her, bent over, and held her knees with her hands.

She might not be safe there, but she was safer than she was before.

"Problems?" Jesse asked from the mirror.

Nora had no words for him. She fell in a heap and didn't care that Jesse was there, watching her cry on the floor.

CHAPTER FOURTEEN

FAKE NORA

Fake Nora had almost made it an entire day as Nora, and she thought it had gone pretty well. Except for the one snafu with Nora's mother, thanks to Fake Nora's hunger for fear. She talked herself out of going to church, which would be a problem every week, but she'd deal. And honestly, if she had to do it, she would go. It would hurt, but she would suffer if she wanted to live in the real world. And she did. She wanted to live in the real world where there were feelings, sounds, and fear.

She'd learned a lot about the real world: about indoor plumbing (gross, but effective), television (moving pictures!), refrigerators, stoves, cars … cars that were everywhere. When she'd been Jesse, she had seen a few cars. Not very many. And they puttered around. Not like the speed demons outside the Williams' house.

So, all in all, she considered it a successful day.

A popping sound on the wooden floor next to her door got her attention. She rolled over in time to see Nora's little brother hiding in the shadows, hugging a little dinosaur stuffed animal.

Fear radiated off him like a lovely snack. She imagined it would be like cake would taste to a human. Only better, because cake was nasty, but she knew Jesse loved cake. Martha, too. The others … the others she couldn't remember. Jesse had a bit of a sweet tooth if she remembered correctly, and Martha … Martha liked sweet candy. At least, that's what Fake Nora assumed they liked. It's what people brought her when they thought she was having problems, to cheer her up and such. It didn't help. Only made everything worse, because she wasn't them. She was her … always living a life of someone else. Never being able to be herself again. Fake Nora forgot what she even looked like, the real her. It had been so long.

She shook her head, not wanting to dwell on those horrible thoughts. It was her first day out of a mirror in so long, and she wanted to enjoy it.

Which meant she wanted to toy with the little brother some.

Fake Nora sat up in her bed and pulled the covers up to her chin. "Can I help you?"

Nora's brother slunk back into the shadows, hugging his dinosaur tighter. Imagine, someone needing a doll to make them feel brave. Gauging from the fear filling her stomach from Nora's little brother, the dinosaur wasn't helping much at all.

"I … I couldn't sleep."

"Well, go back to bed and try again." Fake Nora had no time for such foolishness. If it weren't for his fear giving her a nice snack, she wouldn't entertain him at all. She'd shoo him away like she knew Nora had to have done because her little brother was annoying. Roll over and go to sleep.

As it was, Nora's little brother was feeding her need, so she allowed herself to talk to him. She bet he wished he hadn't bothered in a few minutes.

"I … I can't. I'm scared."

I noticed, Fake Nora wanted to say, but she didn't. "There's nothing in your room that can hurt you." 'Cause I'm in here, she thought to herself and tried to hide a grin. It must not have worked, because she was pretty sure Nora's little brother saw it. He jumped into the shadows a little deeper.

"What's wrong with you, Nora?" His brave little voice broke as he spoke.

"Nothing. What's wrong with you?" She inhaled his fear, loving every single second of it.

"I'm scared," he said once more.

"Scared of what?" She had a feeling she knew, but she wanted him to say it. It made it so much better when they said it.

"I'm scared ... I'm scared of you." Fake Nora couldn't help it. She roared with laughter. Laughed so loud, Nora's mother yelled up the stairs to see what was going on. "Nothing. Nol ... I mean, my little brother got up scared, and I'm trying to make him feel better."

"Do I need to come up there?" Nora's mother shouted, not unkindly.

"Yes," Nora's little brother said at the same time Fake Nora said, much louder, "No."

Nora's little brother's bottom lip trembled.

"Okay then, guys. Go to sleep. I love you."

"Love you, too." Fake Nora answered with a smirk, not taking her eyes off of Nora's little brother, who had been reduced to white eyes in the darkness.

"L ... Love you, too," he barely got out, and the words most certainly didn't go downstairs.

"What are you?" he whispered in Fake Nora's direction.

Her eyes narrowed as she glared at the little gnat. He had been fun for a while, but not if he threatened to send her back into the mirror. Fake Nora sat up straight in her bed. Nora's little brother tried to run, but Fake Nora was faster. She grabbed him by the back of the shirt, covered his mouth with her hand, and drug him into Nora's bedroom, locking the door behind them.

Nora's little brother tried to scream and wriggle away, but Fake Nora pulled him closer and only said two words, two words that made him stop in his tracks. "She'll die."

With those words, Nora's little brother tensed, but he stopped fighting. Fake Nora turned him around and motioned for him to be quiet. Nora's little brother put his hand over his mouth to not say a word. "Good boy. Are you ready to listen? Nod if you are."

Nora's little brother nodded.

This wasn't exactly how Fake Nora wanted today to go. She had hoped for a few more days of simply scaring him before all of this had to happen, but she supposed she never really got what she wanted, did she?

"Nora?" Nora's little brother said through his hands. She could tell in his little eyes that he wanted it to be his sister, that he was trying so hard to figure it out. Fake Nora wasn't sure what to tell him. Should she tell him it was a joke? That she wanted to scare him, but it had gone too far, and she was sorry now? Should she tell him the truth? Well, not exactly the truth, because that wouldn't be good. She could tell him a version of the truth. She could say … Fake Nora's eyes lit up. She figured out what she wanted to tell him, and it was brilliant. It was something that would make sure her identity was secret, and she would have a steady stream of fear rolling in her direction.

And it would almost be the truth.

"Can you keep a secret?" Fake Nora inched closer to Nora's little brother, who backed as far away from her as he could with his little hand over his mouth, until his bottom hit the mattress on the bed, and he sat down with a thump.

"Can you? I need to know." Fake Nora squatted down in front of him, inhaling his fear. It tasted so good.

He nodded adamantly, and Fake Nora did her best to smile compassionately at the young man. He could be useful. "I'm not really your sister."

Nora's little brother scooted back, his eyes wide. She held up her hands to steady him, without touching him. She didn't want him to be too afraid, though it would be tasty. "But I'm not going to hurt you, okay? I'm not. Nora, she's gone somewhere far away."

"Where?" came his little voice from behind his hand.

"Far, far away. And the people who have her, they work for me." As good of a lie as any. "And if you tell your parents about me not being Nora, they will do something horrible to her."

"Horrible?" His eyes filled with tears.

"Horrible. Do you want that to happen to your sister?"

He shook his head no.

"Do you want to be the reason something bad happens to Nora?"

Again, he shook his head adamantly no.

"No, I didn't think so. So, this is what we are going to do. I won't be here long." Another lie. "If you play your part, but if you try to tell your parents that I'm not Nora, they will hurt your sister. Do you understand?"

He nodded yes while Fake Nora enjoyed his fearful treat.

"Good."

Nora's little brother moved his hand from his mouth slightly so Fake Nora could hear his words. "She'll be back, though? Nora will be back?"

Never. "As long as you play your part, then yes. She will be back. It's up to you ... Brother."

"Nolan." He corrected her, then covered his mouth again like he might have done the wrong thing.

"Nolan." Fake Nora said with as much compassion as she could muster, which wasn't much. At least, she tried.

"Good. Good talk." She moved out of the way and allowed Nora's little ... Nolan to get off the bed and head toward the locked door.

"Hey, Nolan?" He turned toward her, and when he did, Fake Nora unhinged her jaw, so her mouth contorted in a horrible angle. She rolled her tongue up like a spiral and rolled her eyes in the back of her head. With her eyes at that angle, she couldn't see anything, but she sure heard it. Nolan scratched at the door, turning and turning the knob, unable to unlock it.

She rolled her eyes back down, fixed her face, and slammed her hand next to Nolan before he could open the door. "Remember what I told you."

She scratched in his ear, perfectly pure fear rolling off him in waves. "You tell, and she dies."

Nodding several times, Nolan watched her as tears rolled down his face. Fake Nora opened the door for him, and Nolan ran out the door and into his room where he hid under the covers.

Well, it was one way to deal with it.

Fake Nora climbed back under her covers and rested her gaze back on the ceiling. "Good night … Nolan." She called through the house, just to test him.

He didn't answer.

"I said, good night, Nolan," she said again, this time with a bit of anger in her voice.

"G—Goodnight," he answered back, making her kick with laughter. She felt energized by how well she was being fed with the little brat's fear. She'd been wrong about this place. She'd definitely made the right decision coming here. She didn't have to scare the parents, and the little brother would be a feast for years to come.

Life was good.

Fake Nora placed her hands behind her head with a content smile across her face.

Life was so … so good.

CHAPTER FIFTEEN

NORA

"Well, that was a quick trip." Jesse had an *I told you so* tone to his voice.

Nora didn't want to hear it, nor did she feel like speaking to him.

"How long are you planning on lying there and crying?" Jesse asked with a sigh.

"Does it matter? I thought time means nothing here." Nora sniffled, wiping the tears away with the back of her hand as she felt all the weight of her situation cover her. If she couldn't even get downstairs, how would she get out the door? And would the door even lead her home? Was Jesse right, and there was no hope?

"It doesn't, but that doesn't mean I want to hear

you crying for the rest of eternity." Jesse sounded grumpy. Nora felt grumpy so they could be all grumpy together.

"Then talk to me and make me feel better about life." Nora propped her head on her hands, still lying on the floor. Water from her tears saturated her long sleeves. Despite the uncomfortable feeling, Nora didn't care. She had so many other things on her mind that wet sleeves were the least of her worries.

"I don't know anything about life," Jesse answered most unhelpfully.

"Make something up, then." If he could just talk, talk about anything that wasn't this house or reflections, or anything remotely scary or sad, she would greatly appreciate it. She wasn't sure what a boy from the forties could talk about that she would understand, but she would do her best to follow along because it wouldn't have to do with the house or bad ones. That's all she cared about at the moment.

"I don't have a great imagination." Jesse sighed, and Nora nearly resigned herself to the fact that he wasn't going to say anything when Jesse finally spoke. "I was born in nineteen twenty-seven. I'm the youngest of seven kids."

"Easy to remember." Twenty-seven. Seven kids.

"Sometimes. Sometimes it feels like I could just run upstairs, and my brothers and sisters would be there with me. Most of the time, though, I know I'm alone. Well, as alone as you can be with the bad ones running around."

"Don't talk about bad ones, please. Just, nice things. Nice ... please." Nora wasn't beyond begging at this point. If he could talk to her, ease her fears, she would be grateful forever. If he could do that for her, she would be happy to repay him anytime he wanted to hear a story about the future. And seeing as she didn't think she'd ever leave the room again, it would probably be her turn to talk very soon.

"Nice things." Jesse took a few seconds to think. "My mother smelled like lavender perfume."

Nora smiled and closed her eyes, imagining Jesse in his old house with his brothers and sisters, his parents sitting around the fire in the living room. His mother probably sewed while sitting by the fire. His father probably read the paper with the radio on. The kids did ... whatever kids did in the forties.

Jesse went on. "Every year, my father would buy her a bottle of it for her birthday. We didn't have much. Well, we had more than a lot of people, but we didn't have money for extra things. Ma loved that lavender perfume, and Pa would make sure every year she had it for her birthday. Same with us kids. We wore clothes that were handed down. Ma fixed the holes in them and all. On our birthday, though, Pa would get us something special. Maybe a piece of candy from the store. Or even a birthday cake. Once, he bought me an orange. An orange! All for me. Can you imagine?"

Nora laid her head down on her wet sleeve, feeling a bit guilty about not being grateful for an orange. It seemed so strange for someone to be so excited about something that her mother had sitting on their table every day.

"Nora, are you there?" Jesse asked when she hadn't answered his question.

"Sounds nice," she said, and she meant it. The way he told the story did sound nice, and his father sounded like an incredibly kind and generous man. "What did your father do for a living?"

"He was a farmer when I was younger. Then, we moved to this house in the city, and he started working at the factory. Lots of my friends, their pas did the same thing. Just kind of happened, I guess. He made more money, but I don't think he was happier. I think he missed the farm. I know I missed it. I still miss it." His voice dropped. Nora felt bad that she had brought up so many painful memories. She'd wanted him to talk to her because she wanted to feel better about being away from her parents. And here she was making him think about his past and how much he must miss his own family.

"I'm sorry. I shouldn't bring it up." She tried to change the subject, but Jesse stopped her.

"No, it's fine. I haven't had anyone to talk to about them. Not in so long. Ever, actually, in here."

"Martha didn't listen?"

"Martha was almost too far gone when I got here. She talked in long-winded stories that made no sense in circles that kept going around and around with no end, no point. It was like she was trying to talk so she'd be whole, so she wouldn't forget. Then one day ..."

"One day, what?"

"She forgot," he answered gloomily. "She forgot. She just stopped talking, and I watched her. I watched as the light faded from her eyes like she'd given up completely, and she knew she was never getting out of here. There's a difference between knowing you won't get out and accepting it. I know, but I guess I haven't accepted it. Martha did. She just stopped talking, closed her eyes, and I watched her as she disappeared. Just vanished. Then the wind picked up, and I felt something … I felt her fly by me. She became one of them. One of the bad ones. I've been in this room ever since. They don't come in here."

"Why?"

"I don't know. I don't know the rules here. All I know is the bad ones are bad news."

"I found that out myself." Nora sighed; they were back to talking about the bad ones. All roads lead to them. "How long was Martha here before she turned into a bad one?"

"She said she was born before the Civil War. She said before the war, her pa made her ma a dresser with an old mirror he'd found in a field. The mirror is where she first saw her reflection that wasn't her reflection."

The dresser! It had to have been the same one they'd bought at the antique store! "You had it, too, right?"

"Yes. My pa bought it for my ma. Why? Do you have it now?"

"I do. We bought it Saturday."

"Interesting. What does it mean?" Jesse asked with a little hope in his voice.

"I have no idea." Nora laid her head down on the floor, not too hot, not too cold. "I just don't know."

CHAPTER SIXTEEN

FAKE NORA

Life in the Williams' house wasn't terrible for Fake Nora. The family lifestyle was way more peaceful than any other house she'd live in during her life. Even her recent home, Jesse's home, was full of waking up at dawn, doing menial chores, going to bed at sundown. It had been that way for Fake Nora her entire life, even from the time she was a child, when she was human. Though she supposed her own mother would question if Fake Nora ever was human.

It was Saturday, and Fake Nora had been in the Williams family for almost a week. Nora's little brother, Nolan, supplied her with all the fear she could ever want. She slipped up a few times with

Nora's parents, calling them the wrong names, not knowing how to get clothes out of a dryer ... not knowing what a dryer was. But slowly, Fake Nora picked up on the modern terminology and began settling into her new role. In fact, Fake Nora found herself liking it in the Williams' house. Nora's mother proved to be a kind woman who liked to garden, didn't raise her voice at her kids, and liked to sew—actually sew for fun, not sew as in what Fake Nora's mother had to do when she was growing up. Or Nora had to do in Martha's household, or so many of the other households through the ages.

Fake Nora also liked Nora's father. He went to work every day, came home smiling every night, never raising a hand to either Nora or her brother. He kissed Nora's mother on the top of the head when he came home, and Fake Nora heard them laughing in their room while a television played softly in the background late into the night.

Then there was Nolan, Nora's little brother. Nolan provided Fake Nora with all the food she needed to live, all the fear she craved. He hadn't said anything to their parents about Fake Nora being fake, which was good. He was convinced Fake Nora would kill real Nora if he did. Little did the boy know Fake Nora had no control over what happened to the reflections inside the mirror.

She knew what happened to them, of course. By trading lives with Fake Nora, mostly not by their choice, the reflections were stuck in a bit of a purgatory, a place where they couldn't leave—they couldn't die, they couldn't live. They were simply there, as she had been. Until they got to do something Fake Nora never could, or at least she didn't think she could. They would disappear, vanish and become the bad ones. Fake Nora shivered when she thought of the bad ones. Even someone like her, someone who fed on fear and was called evil most of her life, feared the bad ones and what they might be able to do to her. They were all mad at her, that was for sure, and if she thought hard enough, Fake Nora would realize they had a reason to be mad at her. She was the one who sent them there, after all, to become a reflection, something that wasn't even able to interact with anyone ever again.

Except ... when they could.

It was a lazy Saturday. Nora's mother told her they'd go on their weekly trip after she tended to the garden. Fake Nora had no idea what their weekly trip entailed, but she looked forward to spending time with Nora's mother. And as scared as Nora's little brother stayed constantly, Fake Nora had a full belly and knew she could stay away from the source of her food for a while and not suffer.

She was also curious, curious how Nora was doing inside the mirror. Had she turned into a bad one yet? Most reflections didn't in such a short amount of time. Fake Nora was curious, though. Sometimes, her mother would say she was too curious, and that got her into trouble. Fake Nora didn't believe in such things. How could one be too curious? She'd learned so much after what happened with Jesse that she knew she'd never be stuck inside a mirror again. So confident was she, that she broke her own rule, one she'd come up with after Jesse's father banished her inside that horrible mirror and went to the guest room.

Fake Nora closed her eyes as she walked toward the dresser, not ready to look inside the glass. She would look for a second. Only a second. Then it would be over. She'd check on Nora. Make sure Nora knew her life was going great, and her family didn't miss her, and then Fake Nora would leave the room. Easy as that.

Once her outstretched fingers hit solid wood, Fake Nora took a deep breath and slowly, very slowly, opened her eyes. No reflection met her.

In fact, the reflection was the same as it was before, bland, nothing, and Fake Nora recognized it immediately. This was how it looked when she'd been inside the mirror, and a covering had been placed on it. Placed over it by Jesse's family so Fake Nora could never get out. That lasted until Nora's mother bought the mirror, and the rest was history.

"Nora." Fake Nora whispered into the glass. "Nora Williams? Where are you?"

It might be easier to get a response if she tapped on the glass, but no way was Fake Nora going to do that. She might look in the mirror for a short length of time. There was no way she'd touch the glass. Things that ate fear feared things as well, and Fake Nora feared the mirror.

Still, curiosity and all. Fake Nora called for Nora once more. "I know you're in there, Nora. Where else would you go? Come to the mirror, take the covering off so I can see you? Come on ... unless you want your brother hurt."

Fake Nora waited with a smile pulling on her lips. She knew Nora would come now. Her own curiosity would draw her like a moth to the flame.

CHAPTER SEVENTEEN

NORA

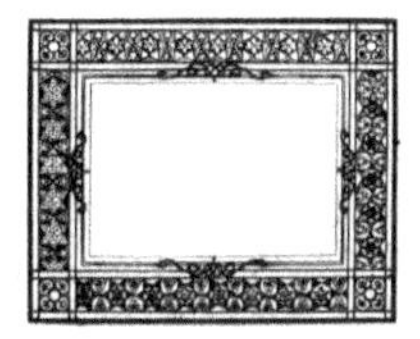

Nora had no idea how long she'd been lying there on the floor of the bathroom, and honestly, she didn't care. Jesse was right: time didn't matter there. Nothing mattered there. It was neither hot nor cold, sunny nor dark. Even her stomach felt strange. She was hungry, but not painfully so. A big chicken dinner sounded amazing, but the feeling of hunger didn't cause her any physical discomfort.

It would be assumed that Nora would need to eat. So far, she hadn't. She hadn't gone to the bathroom, brushed her teeth, or done any of the simple things of being human. All she did was lay on the bathroom floor. Sometimes, she thought. Sometimes, she pushed all thoughts out of her mind and simply stared at a tile on the floor for no telling how long. Sometimes, she talked to Jesse, though their conversations were few and far between.

Far away, as if in some other part of the world, Nora heard her name being called. And the strange part was, the voice calling it sounded a lot like her.

Assuming her mind played tricks on her, Nora ignored the sound and settled against the floor once more, staring under the sink into a little hole where nothing ever went in, and nothing ever went out.

She heard her name once more, this time louder and clearer. Nora sat up and looked around the room. "Did you say that?" she asked Jesse, though she knew it couldn't have been him. He had a deep voice, almost as deep as a man's. And this voice calling her name was most definitely a girl's.

"No," he answered without any other reply.

His curt answer worried Nora, and she sat up on her knees, then her feet. She assumed she'd be stiff or sore from lying down on the floor for so long. Her bones felt fine, no stiffness at all. The reflection world was great for one thing, no pain.

Nora's smile faded, however, when she looked in the mirror over the sink and saw Jesse. He lay down on the couch at the far end of the room, his arm drawn over his eyes. Normally, he paced a lot, even if he wasn't talking. In all the times Nora had gazed in the mirror, she'd never seen him lying down, which might not have meant anything. "You okay?"

"Fine."

"You don't look fine."

"I'm fine." He sounded very much not fine. His voice cracked as he spoke. "I promise. I'm fine," he answered a little softer. "Just got tired of standing, so I'm lying down. Is lying down a crime in the future?"

"No." Nora felt bad for asking Jesse if he was okay for simply lying down. Of course, it wasn't bad to lie down. It was just ... hearing her name had made her jumpy.

"Good." Jesse sighed. "And no, I didn't hear your name."

"Think it was all in my head?"

"I think there's a lot of things going on inside our heads," he answered cryptically.

"I think ..." And before she could tell him what she thought, she heard her name once more, like a dull echo, since the house didn't have echoes.

Nora turned toward Jesse, who moved his arm from his eyes. "I heard that."

"So, I'm not crazy."

"Didn't say that. I just said I heard it. I wouldn't go looking for the source, though."

"It could be my mother," Nora said hopefully. She hadn't had hope in so long, so, so long, and the feeling nearly consumed her. To go from no feelings to all the feelings, so strong and powerful, practically knocked her backwards.

In fact, it did knock her backwards. She staggered until her back hit the wall beside the bathtub. She grabbed her chest to keep her heart from exploding from all the wonderful emotions running through her. Her mother missed her! She was looking for her, and, once her feet would carry her again, Nora would go find her.

"I know that look." Jesse sat up and rolled off the couch. "Don't trust it, Nora. Don't think that's your mother, because it's not."

"It is." Nora barely got the words out, so excited that she would be home soon. Home with smells, with macaroni and cheese, with her little brother annoying her … home with the smells of her mother cooking, her dad mowing the yard, her hair after she washed it. She'd be home soon, and she would try her best to get Jesse out, too. She wouldn't forget him, but she had to go, and go now …

"It's probably the bad ones." Jesse walked

toward the mirror like he was trying to calm a wild animal. Nora hated to tell him it wouldn't do any good. She had her mind made up.

"It's not. They sounded different. And we haven't heard them in so long. It's my mom, Jesse. I know it is."

"And I know it isn't."

Tears sprang to Nora's eyes. "Why do you have to be so negative, Jesse?"

"I'm not being negative. I'm being realistic. I'm telling you the truth. Something is calling your name—"

"So you heard it?"

Jesse kept on going like she hadn't said anything. "But that something isn't your mother. It's not, and you getting your hopes up will only end badly. I can promise you that. Trust me."

Nora had heard enough. She wasn't going to be like Jesse and be okay living the rest of her life as a reflection in a mirror. Anger, another strong emotion, filled her, and she stood straight, shoulders back, her eyes straight ahead. "I don't know you well enough to trust you."

She reached for the door handle, all the while Jesse yelling at her to stop. She pulled it open and saw the hallway for the first time in so long. It hadn't changed at all. Dim, like it had been before. Dim and void. The same things sat in there, same furniture, same everything, only it was like a copy on a copy machine. Sometimes at school, her teacher would make a copy of a copy. That copy of a copy is what the house looked like: washed out, dim, not full of life or color.

"Nora!" The voice called, and Nora knew instantly the sound came from the guest room. It made sense since that room was where the mirror sat, and the mirror was how she'd gotten into the world anyway.

"Mama!" Nora yelled as she ran down the hallway and through the door to the guest room. She raced to the dresser and yanked the covering off the mirror, expecting to see her mother.

Praying to see her mother.

Instead, she was met with the reflection of herself, or rather, she saw a copy of herself, smiling back at her.

She looked exactly like Nora, just as she had when hiding in the doorframe when she'd seen her last time. This … Fake Nora … she was a good copy; Nora gave her that. She had the same red hair color, same pale skin color, same blue eye color, same short height … but there was something very off about her, something behind the eyes that Nora noticed wasn't human. How could her family think that Fake Nora was her? There was no way. They had to know, right?

Right?

Nora started to ask a question when Fake Nora's hand shot up over her head. As if being pulled by a puppet string, Nora's hand did the exact same movement, at the exact same time. Like she was a reflection with no will of her own.

Fake Nora smiled in the glass, and Nora felt her lips parting in the same way.

"Hello," Fake Nora said, which caused Nora's mouth to move. Even sound came out, repeating—at the same time—what Fake Nora spoke.

She truly was a reflection, a reflection in a mirror, doing whatever the person was doing. Only she wasn't a reflection. She was a person. She wasn't supposed to be here.

Fake Nora crossed her arms. Nora mirrored the movement. It felt so strange for her body to move and her not be the one who did it. Was this what Fake Nora had lived through?

"I don't have much time. Just wanted to check on you. Like your new accommodations?"

Nora tried very hard to open her mouth of her

own free will after Fake Nora's words came out. She found she couldn't do it. She couldn't move at all unless Fake Nora allowed her to.

"Interesting." Fake Nora—and Nora—said at the same time. "I'll tell you how I'm doing. I'm doing wonderful. Your family is so nice, especially your little brother. He keeps me fed."

Nora's mind raced at the mention of her brother. Fake Nora better not hurt him, or Nora would do everything in her power to bring her back into Mirrorland for good and make sure she never left.

"How does he keep me fed, you might ask? Well, fear, my dear. Fear keeps me fed, and your brother has so much of it, it's wonderful. I missed it. But do you know what I don't miss? I don't miss being in that mirror. Being a reflection, not being able to move on my own," She ran her hand through her hair, as did Nora. "Eat on my own. Touch anything. And the days went on and on and on with no end. Here, there are ends. And Nora, your family is so kind. I barely have to work or do any chores. Not like Jesse's family. People today have it made, I'll tell ya."

Nora felt the tears spring in her eyes, but they couldn't drop since Fake Nora wasn't crying. A reflection couldn't do anything its person didn't do.

That was why it was a reflection. She felt, though. She felt all the hope leave her, all the hope and trust that she actually would get out of this place.

Seeing Fake Nora in her life, in her house, it sickened her. Nora wanted to be home so bad: see her parents and get her brother away from Fake Nora. Feeding on the fears of a little boy was the worst thing twelve-year-old Nora could imagine.

"Anyway, just wanted to check on you. See how you were. See if the bad ones had gotten you yet, or if you'd turned into one yet." She, and Nora, laughed darkly. "Fun, aren't they? Just a little side-effect of my little prison world. I wouldn't worry too much about them. They're harmless, unless they come after you." She giggled.

Nora tried with everything she had to ball up her fist and slam it through the mirror. She might not do anything to Fake Nora, but it would make her feel good.

"Off to go antique shopping with your mother. Bye, Nora." Fake Nora wriggled her fingers at her as a good-bye, and movement in the mirror caught her attention. It was a quick movement next to the door so she couldn't truly recognize what it was. Or who it was. Fake Nora turned, as did Nora, who had no choice. The farther away Nora got from the mirror, the less like a puppet she felt. Once she felt the strings releasing, she ran back into the room and covered the mirror with the comforter again. Once it was covered, she ran from the room and down the hallway. Her name bounced around in her head, from voices that weren't her own. They weren't echoes since the house didn't have echoes, but they were there, nonetheless. Voices …

The bad ones.

Nora ran as fast as her legs would take her, her name bouncing through her brain.

Nora …

Nora …

Nora …

Nora …

Male voice.

Female voice.

Nora …

Nora …

Child's voice.

Nora …

Nora …

She bounced off the bathroom door when she got to it and struggled to push the door open.

Nora …

Nora …

Nora!

Her name became longer, more drawn out, more contorted until it sounded more like a horrible word in an ancient language than her actual name.

A feeling came over her, a feeling that something was coming up the steps after her. Out of the corner of her eye, she swore she saw movement. Not wanting to look anymore, she tried with everything she had to open that bathroom door.

Contorted sounds of her name …

Contorted laughter …

Muffled voices repeating the same word over …

And over …

And over …

The skin prickled on her arms as whatever it was, the bad ones most likely, came closer to her, taunting her, calling her with their horrible language.

Without a second to lose, just as she felt the wind from an unseen force swipe at her, Nora forced the bathroom door to open. She fell inside and locked the door behind her. Out of breath and shaking, Nora backed away from the door, keeping her eyes on the handle to see if it moved or shifted. Where would she go if the bad ones decided to come into the bathroom? She had no idea. The only things in there were the window—which was two stories up—and the mirror. That was it.

Nora shook, not allowing herself to blink as her eyes stayed trained on that doorknob, which still hadn't moved.

"Problems?" Jesse asked from the mirror.

Nora didn't even chance a glance at him. She could only keep her eyes on the door. Only on the door.

"Nora?" Jesse asked again, this time with what seemed like concern in his voice. "What did you see out there?"

"N—nothing," Nora answered, her voice shaking. She'd gone from feeling nothing to feeling everything in a few short minutes, and her brain didn't know how to process it.

"You saw nothing? Oh, the bad ones."

She didn't need to nod. Jesse already knew.

"And the voice? Was it your mother?"

He already knew it wasn't, so why did he want to ask?

"Was it the other Jesse?"

"Is that what—what you called it? The other Jesse?" She tried to breathe, to calm herself down. Feeling lightheaded, Nora sat on the toilet seat but kept her eyes trained on the door just in case.

"What else would I call it? What do you call it?"

"Fake Nora."

Jesse laughed lightly. "I like it. It fits."

"What is she?" Nora asked the question she'd wondered for so long but hadn't asked. "What is she, and where did she come from?"

It took a second for Jesse to answer. It took so long that Nora chanced it and took a quick look in his direction to make sure he was still there. He was.

He stood closer to the mirror, his arm resting on what she assumed was the mantel over the fireplace. Jesse's face was downcast, sad. "I don't know what it is. Not really. I always thought it was a demon. A devil. A thing. I stopped trying to figure out what it was when I came to the realization …" he stopped speaking.

"The realization of what?" Did she really want to know?

"When I came to the realization that it didn't matter what it was."

"Doesn't matter?" Nora stood up, prepared to fight. Then her legs nearly gave way, and she grabbed hold of the sink to keep from falling. Looking into the mirror, she was the closest she'd ever been to Jesse. He was right there, as close to the mirror as he could be, and so was she. So close she could reach out and touch it if she wanted, except she was terrified to do that. She didn't want to do it. However, she wanted him to understand why she needed to know what Fake Nora was and why she had no idea why he didn't. "Of course, it matters. It matters."

"Why?" he challenged.

Why? Did he seriously not know?

"Because if we don't know what she is, we can't defeat her."

Jesse rolled his eyes.

"I'm serious, Jesse. I refuse to stay in this place forever. I can't do it. And after seeing her again, it made me even more determined that I'm not staying. I miss my house. I miss my family."

"And you don't think I do?" Jesse's head tilted back, and Nora saw the redness in his eyes. Would he start crying?

"I think you've been here a long time, and you've given up. But I'm here to tell you that you don't have to give up. We can help each other. We can. We can help each other get out, and to do that, we need to know what we're facing."

"And I'm telling you, it doesn't matter. We are here, Nora. We aren't leaving, and the sooner you get that through your brain, the happier you'll be."

"Happy, like you?" She couldn't stop the bite in her voice. It was one thing to be negative, but to be negative when someone was trying to save you was unacceptable.

"That's low."

"I call it like I see it." Even though Nora felt a little bad about what she'd said.

"And so do I." Jesse stood straighter. "I see a little girl who has no idea what she's doing. I see a little girl who doesn't know when she's defeated and doesn't know when to stop."

"Exactly. I know not to give up. And neither can you. Come on, Jesse. What else do you have to do with your days? Help me brainstorm this."

"I don't know what that means."

Nora forgot at times that Jesse wasn't from her time period. "Let's sit down and think, rationally, about what Fake Nora might be and ways we can stop her."

"It's a waste of time."

"Time is all we've got."

Jesse sighed and ran his fingers through his hair.

"Come on, Jesse. You have to be tired in there, and there has to be something in you that wants out, that has a little bit of hope. If not, why did you throw rocks to get my attention? Why did you draw me into the bathroom to keep you company? Why did you warn me about the bad ones?"

He didn't answer.

"If you've given up so much, why help me?"

Nothing.

"What else do you have to do with your time?"

"When you put it that way." Jesse didn't smile, but it was the answer Nora was looking for.

She danced in a circle. When she stopped, she saw Jesse trying to hide a smile. "This will only end in heartbreak, you know that, right?"

"As long as we're doing something to get out of here, it can only end well."

"I hope you're right." Jesse crossed his arms. "I hope you're right."

CHAPTER EIGHTEEN

FAKE NORA

Feeling pretty good about herself, Fake Nora practically skipped down the hallway toward Nora's room to get ready for her first shopping trip in forever. She'd never gone shopping simply to go. She'd gone to the mercantile as Jesse. She'd gone to the blacksmith a few times as Martha. As so many others, she'd gone to local markets on a few days of the month to gather supplies. From what she could tell about this family and this time, people went shopping whenever they wanted and bought ... whatever they wanted.

Instead of going to Nora's room, Fake Nora took a moment to stop by Nora's brother's room. As per usual, he laid with his head covered on his bed, his fear giving her a much-appreciated snack. "So, Nora's brother, I have a question."

At first, Fake Nora didn't think he'd answer her. Then, before she could ask again, he said, "Nolan. My name is Nolan."

He kept telling her his name, like it mattered, and Fake Nora kept forgetting it, because it didn't. "Yes, Nolan, Nora's brother. I have a question, and only you can answer it."

He sat up on his bed, but the covers still covered him. He looked like a ghost on Halloween. All he needed was eyes cut out of the white blanket to see, and he'd be ready to go boo. "You need to ask me something?" He seemed a bit bewildered by that. Fake Nora supposed it was because in the last, oh, week, she'd never done anything to him besides make horrible smiling faces to amp up his fear. She'd never actually talked to him since that first day, which didn't bother her. She didn't care if it bothered him.

"Yes, and believe me, I'm not one to talk to my dinner, so you must know that this is an important thing I'm asking."

"O—kay."

Fake Nora cleared her throat. "What is ... an antique store?"

Nora's brother laughed. He actually laughed, guffawed even. Fake Nora couldn't understand what she had said that was so funny. "Do you not know what it is?"

"No, I know."

"Then why do you laugh? Is it something scandalous? Is it strange that Nora's mother is taking me?"

Nora's brother's laughter faded at the mention of his mother. "It's Saturday, huh?"

"It is."

"Nora and Mama always go to the antique store on Saturday. It's where they got that stupid mirror."

"Ah ..." Fake Nora didn't see the connection between Saturday and shopping, nor did she understand what an antique store was yet. "So, what does that mean?"

"Don't you know everything or whatever?"

It was Fake Nora's turn to scoff. "I'm not God, silly. I don't know everything."

The cover fell from his head, and Nora's brother glared at her. "Then, what are you?"

"What am I? I'm your sister." She smirked.

Nora's brother was having none of it. "No, you're not. You're something bad. I want you to go away, and I want my sister back. And I want to know what you are!"

"Careful, yelling like that," Fake Nora warned. "Your parents will hear you, and then Nora will be hurt. Do you want Nora hurt because of you?"

"No." He hung his head.

"Good, then you'd better remember that I'm the one asking the questions here. Not you. I don't owe you any explanation except since I'm so kind, I will tell you one thing. At one time, I was human, like you. I had a mother who loved me. Then …"

"Then?" His big eyes looked at Fake Nora with some kind of hope inside them that maybe she'd tell him something that would help his sister. Or maybe he was simply curious. In any case, it kept Fake Nora from telling him what truly happened.

Instead, she said, "Then she didn't."

"That's sad," Nora's brother answered, confusing her.

"Why is that sad? I'm evil. I'm bad. You aren't supposed to feel bad for bad people."

He shrugged, and his shoulders fell. "I'm sure you weren't always bad. And I'm sure your mom just didn't know what she was doing."

Well, that little monster.

Fake Nora stood straighter, ignoring the strange

pulling close to her heart that might … might … feel a little fondness for the boy. “In any case, it is what it is. And I would like to know exactly what an antique store is.”

He stared at her.

“Now, you little brat.”

Nora’s little brother jumped and pulled the covers up to his chest. “It’s a place, a place where you buy old things.”

Fake Nora had to have heard him wrong. “People actually … buy … things that are old?”

Nora’s brother nodded.

“But why? Are there no stores for new things in the future?”

“The future?”

“Now,” she grunted, growing tired of the five-year-old. Couldn’t Nora have had an older brother? “Now, are there no new stores now?”

“Yes, but people like my mom like old things.”

“Why?” Fake Nora could not figure it out.

“You’d have to ask her.” He lay back down and pulled the cover up as far as it could go.

Fake Nora decided she’d better go before he said something that sparked some kind of fondness for the boy, and before she accidentally told him something he didn’t need to know about her.

Before she got to the door, Fake Nora turned, taking in the shaking little boy under the covers. "Hey, Nolan?"

Nora's brother smiled when Fake Nora said his real name. Like he'd finally gotten through to her.

Fake Nora twisted her face into a snarl, rolled her eyes in the back of her head, and growled, causing Nora's brother to scream.

She tasted his fear.

It tasted like victory.

CHAPTER NINETEEN

NORA

Nora lay on the floor, staring at the ceiling, thinking. "Ghost?"

"She doesn't seem to be a ghost. She is solid when she goes from place to place, so I don't think that's what she is," Jesse answered. Nora couldn't see him but imagined he was lying down on his couch, staring up at his own ceiling.

"Good point. And bright side, since she's not a ghost, we should easily be able to get rid of her."

"Is there any situation you don't see the bright side of?" Jesse's words were a bit harsh, but his tone was playful.

"No," she answered, matter of fact. "Now, come on. What theory do you have? You've had way longer to think about this than I have."

"Ummm … witch?"

"Hmmm …" Nora pondered the idea. "I don't think so. I think, if she were a witch, she would enjoy what she's doing more. She seems like she's upset about having to live someone else's life. She seems like she'd rather be herself. And she most certainly didn't like it in the mirror."

"I didn't like it when she was in here, either." Nora heard the shudder in Jesse's voice.

"She was in here with you?"

"Where else would she be? She was in her own mirror world, or whatever you want to call it. I could have talked to her if I wanted. I didn't want to. She ruined my life, stole it away from me. I sure didn't want to have anything to do with her. But she liked to taunt me, sing to me, tell me how she hurt my family."

"She told me she'd hurt my little brother." Nora's fist balled up when she thought about it. She wanted to hit whatever Fake Nora was in the nose for threatening her brother.

"She's a fun one." Jesse sighed. "What else you got?"

Nora thought and thought. "Vampire?"

"Unless it's a fear vampire." Jesse laughed

darkly. He meant it as a joke, but Nora sat straight up.

"You're a genius!"

"Me?"

Nora stood and looked in Jesse's mirror. Once she did, she saw that she'd been wrong about him. He wasn't lying down like her at all. He was pacing the floor, back and forth, biting his thumbnail. His hair laid haphazardly all around his head. Jesse didn't gaze up at the mirror to see her. That worried her.

"Yeah, you. You figured it out."

He didn't stop. He kept pacing, walking faster and faster, gnawing on his thumbnail. "Figured out what? What did I figure out?"

"Fake Nora, or The Other Jesse, or whatever we are calling it, it's a fear vampire."

"That's … the dumbest thing I've ever heard."

"Is it? 'Cause I think it's brilliant."

"You would." He mumbled under his breath.

"Think about it. She said she fed on my brother because he was afraid of her. She lives by eating fear by draining it out of people or whatever she does. So that means, fear vampire."

"What about living in mirrors? What about being a reflection? Wouldn't that make her more of a … what do you call it … when something looks like someone else?"

"Doppelgänger?" Nora said, proud she remembered that word from her fourth-grade reading book last year. She could even spell it.

"Yeah, doppelgänger. What if she's one of those?"

"Hmmm … A fear-eating vampire doppelgänger?" Nora rolled the idea over in her mind. "That does sound like it covers all the bases."

Jesse smiled at the mirror, then his body shook violently. He hunched over to try to cover the movement, but it didn't work. Nora saw the strain of his face, the way his body twisted and contorted.

"Jesse?" She reached for the mirror, then stopped herself. She didn't know what would happen if she touched another mirror. It might make things worse than it already was. She didn't want that. She wanted to help Jesse, though. "Are you okay?"

"Fine, Sunshine." He smiled at her through gritted teeth. "Gonna take more than this to get rid of me."

The words sank into Nora's heart as the realization consumed her. "You're fading, aren't you? You're turning into a bad one."

Instead of his typical snarky reply, Jesse simply looked at her. He had fear in his eyes. Fear and sadness. "Got a positive thing to say about that?"

She wished she did. More than anything, she wished she could think of a positive to make him feel better. "I don't want you to go away," she said instead. It was the absolute truth. She'd lost everything, everyone, and even though she had every intention of getting out of there, she didn't want to think about doing it without Jesse. He was the one person she could talk to in this entire place. If she lost him, she didn't know what she'd do.

"I don't either, Sunshine," Jesse said.

"Why did you start calling me Sunshine?"

He hugged himself tightly as she looked at her. "Because you see the light in everything, the positive. I don't know, I think it fits. Besides, my Nana's name is Nora." He chuckled slightly.

Nora tried to keep the tears from rolling. She'd never had a nickname before. Most kids had, she supposed, but she just hadn't. She'd always been Nora, and now she was Jesse's Sunshine. It made her not want him to leave her that much more.

"What did you say Martha did before, to keep herself from changing into a bad one?"

"It doesn't matter. She changed, so obviously it

didn't help, but thanks for bringing her up." He rolled his eyes and turned his back to Nora.

She sighed, not giving up. "It worked for a little while. You said she talked, a lot. Talked in circles, talked about everything. That's what you need to do. You need to talk. Talk my ear off."

He shook his head at every word Nora said. "No. I don't talk that much. I don't have much to say."

"You have to," Nora said stubbornly. "You have to talk and talk fast, so you stay here with me. I'm not losing you."

"Aw, didn't know you cared, Sunshine."

"You know what I mean."

His expression sobered. "I know. I just, I guess I don't see the point of delaying the inevitable. I'm going to disappear. Be gone. Turn into one of those evil things, and there's nothing you or I or anybody can do about it. Why delay it? Why not just give into it?"

Nora was horrified. "You can't be serious, can you? You want to give up? You want to just let it take you over without fighting?"

"I'm tired of fighting." He shrugged. "I've been in here a long time. Everyone I know is gone. Even if I do get out, what's out there for me? Nothing. Not my parents. Not my siblings."

"You don't know that."

He smiled without any joy. "I do know, Nora."

He'd said her real name, which broke her heart.

"You don't. We've figured something out. Fake Nora is a fear-eating vampire doppelgänger. We can work with that. We know that where she is, in the real world, it is Saturday."

"We know that?"

"Yes, because she said that she was going antique mall shopping with my mother today. We only do that on Saturdays. Every Saturday, so it has to be Saturday. I've been gone a week. Only a week. We can do this, Jesse. We can. I just need you to fight disappearing, okay? Don't turn into a bad one. Please."

He turned his back to her. "So, what if we know what day it is? How is that going to help anything?"

Nora thought a few seconds. "I don't know, but it's something we know, and it's something we can use to our advantage if we need it. I'm not giving up on us, Jesse. I'm not."

"And how does one defeat a fear-eating vampire doppelgänger?"

Nora opened her mouth ... then shut it ... then

opened it again. Then, it hit her, like a ton of bricks. If she and Jesse were in the same place, she'd hug him. "By getting rid of her food source."

"Her food … fear? You want to get rid of fear?"

Nora felt like she was on a roll. "She has to eat, right? And, by her admission, she eats fear, specifically the fear of my brother. If we can get him to somehow not be afraid of her, then we have a shot."

"One, that's a very long shot, and two, how are you going to talk to your brother?"

"I'll get him to the mirror someway. I'll talk to him. I can do it now! Fake Nora and my mother are gone, right? This is the perfect time to talk to him, draw him to the mirror. If we can get him on our side, we can starve Fake Nora out, and she'll …"

"She'll what?" Jesse asked expectantly.

"She'll … she'll starve. And when she starves, she'll be defeated. Maybe, if she starves and dies, all this will disappear, and we'll be free."

"That's a lot of maybes."

"Do you have any better ideas?" If he did, she'd love to hear them. This plan wasn't the best in the world. Starving a fear vampire doppelgänger wasn't easy, especially in the big, scary world. There was so much fear, everywhere. Every time Nora watched television or turned on the internet, there was so much fear. She had a feeling, though, a good feeling that this would work.

She would arm Nolan with the knowledge that he didn't need to fear Fake Nora. In fact, fearing her would hurt Nora, and he wouldn't want that. Even at five, he would understand. And she'd tell him to tell their parents if needed. She didn't know how they'd take it. Her mom had always been pretty open-minded about things, but this was a bit outside the realm of what was typical, even for her mom. Nora prayed Nolan could get her mother to understand. She also prayed that he could be safe with Fake Nora around. She didn't know what Fake Nora was capable of, and she honestly didn't want to know. Nora knew that they had to be careful with all this: careful with Nolan, with Jesse, with the bad ones, with Fake Nora. So many things could go wrong … but one thing could go right. She could end up back home with her family. It's what she wanted more than anything.

And she wanted Jesse to be all right.

Jesse shook his head. He had no better ideas. That settled it. She would go back to the mirror and try to get Nolan's attention while away from the bad ones. "I'm going to try to talk to my brother. You stay here and don't disappear."

"I'll try."

"Don't try. Do," she scolded him. "You focus, and you keep from disappearing, got me? I need you in that mirror when I come back in here. Do you understand?"

"Yes, ma'am." Jesse grinned with a hint of humor sparkling in his eye.

"Good." With a new determination, Nora marched to the door, tried her best not to think about the bad ones that had chased her into this bathroom to start with, and opened the door.

She didn't have much time.

CHAPTER TWENTY

FAKE NORA

Antique shopping was boring.

So. Incredibly. Boring.

And that was from someone who had been locked in a mirror for almost a hundred years.

Fake Nora didn't get the appeal. All of this stuff was old. People nowadays had machines that made coffee, in their homes! They had refrigerators, electric cars, electric microwaves that cooked things in literally minutes. They had air conditioners, indoor plumbing, televisions! What was the need of an old crank can opener when you could have an electric one? What was the need to have old furniture when you could literally go get something new?

Not that Fake Nora was sad about that one. If Nora's mother didn't love old things so much, she wouldn't have bought her mirror, and, well, things wouldn't have gone the way they had. Fake Nora was glad someone liked antiques. She just didn't herself. She liked new things, shiny things. She'd lived in the old life. In fact, she'd lived several old lives in several time periods all through history. This time was most definitely the easiest. She didn't even have to milk the family cow every morning and night! How was this not the best time in history?

Nora's mother pulled into the small parking lot of an old, rundown shop a few miles away from their house. Fake Nora had gotten used to riding in a car that went incredibly fast. At first, she'd dug her fingers into the seats, but she'd adapted well. That was something she prided herself on, adapting to any situation.

A sign across the porch of the old house read GIBSON'S ANTIQUES. Good to know they knew what they were selling.

Nora's mom cut off the ignition. "Let's see if we can find another steal like we did last week."

Without waiting for a reply, she got out of the car, and Fake Nora followed. Once inside, Nora's mother went her own direction, as did Fake Nora. Gibson's Antiques was the second place they'd visited so far for the day. Nora's mother had mentioned they might hit up five more. Five more … of the same mundane things as the one before.

At least she was out of the house. That was a good thing.

Fake Nora walked around slowly, trying to decipher what in the world someone would want with an old spoon. As she meandered through the twisty rows of old things, she came across a little room in the back. It was narrow, so narrow she could easily touch each side with the tips of her fingertips. A stuffed boar's head had been mounted on the side of the small room, basically a hallway, taking up most of the room. This room had several things that were a bit more interesting than the ones in the main area. There was a black iron bed with a tarp covering it, a lamp that was turned on even though it was unplugged from any outlet Fake Nora saw, and a doll whose eyes seemed to follow her wherever she went.

What was this place?

"Back in here again?" A man's voice boomed behind her, causing her to jump. She greedily slurped up the fear that had escaped her and, once composed, turned toward the voice.

A tall man stood in the entryway to the narrow hallway-like room. He had on overalls with a white shirt underneath. Once Fake Nora turned to face him, his smile faded a bit, replaced with what she took as slight confusion. "You are the girl who was in here last week, weren't you?"

"Yup, that was me." Fake Nora tried to give her best Nora impression, which was over the top and sugary sweet, just as she imagined Nora was all the time to everyone. Kind of annoying.

"You bought the mirror, right?"

Shoot, he remembered. "Well, my mom did."

"Of course, your mom did." The tall man walked toward her a step. "So, how's it going?"

"Oh, you know, life's fine. Summer vacation and all."

"Not that. The mirror. How's the mirror?"

"Fine," she said again, not getting the best vibe from this man.

"Nothing out of the ordinary?"

Fake Nora shook her head and stepped back a step. "No, nothing. Nothing out of the ordinary at all. If you'll excuse me, I should probably be finding my mother." Fake Nora scooted around the man, not liking the look he gave her as she passed.

"You know, my mother always had a fear of that mirror," the man said, making Fake Nora stop in her tracks.

"She did?"

"Yes, she said it was cursed. Never wanted me to sell it, but you know, your mother offered me three times as much as it was worth, and I couldn't let that much money go. Not much money in antiques these days."

Finally, some people in this time had sense. "I don't believe in curses."

"Oh, me either, but that didn't mean I didn't keep it covered, so the evil little thing that lived in it, that stole my mother's brother, didn't get out."

Fake Nora froze. This was Jesse's relation! It would have been so much easier if it had been some random person who had found the mirror or bought the mirror or done something to the mirror.

"You see, my mother, she never lost hope that one day her brother would be brought home."

"Where—where did he go?" Fake Nora knew exactly where he'd gone, more than anyone else in the world, actually. Not that she would admit it to this tall gentleman.

"I don't know. Some people say that something came out of the mirror and swapped places with Jesse. They said that whatever it was tried to take over Jesse's life. It worked for a little bit, but the evil thing wasn't as good at playing pretend as it thought. The family knew it wasn't their son. My mother says it was because the thing didn't have Jesse's spark, his light that made him special. My grandfather put the evil thing back in the mirror but couldn't get Jesse back, so the family kept it covered with a cloth so the evil thing couldn't get back out into the world."

"And you sold it to my mother?" Fake Nora tried to fake shock. "How could you? And all for a dollar."

The tall man shook his head. "I never said I believed any of it. Just saying what the story is. And my mother, she's never given up hope that her brother will find his way home."

Fake Nora's eyes grew dangerously dark, so dangerous that she threatened to expose who she really was to this tall man, more than likely a Gibson since that was the name on the store. Gibson … Jesse Gibson. Just her luck. "You tell your mother that she might as well give up that crusade, because her brother is never coming back."

Mr. Gibson's eyes narrowed as Nora's mother rounded the corner. "Mr. Gibson, I've found some more things. I'm ready to check out now."

"Be right there." Mr. Gibson never stopped glaring at Fake Nora as he walked past her. "Have a good day … ma'am," he said to Fake Nora before turning his back and walking upfront with Nora's mother.

Fake Nora let out a breath she knew she'd been holding and tried to gather her wits. That wasn't how she wanted this to go. Why, of all people, did she have to run into a descendant of that idiot, Jesse? Taking Jesse had been the worst decision of her very long life. It wasn't one she wanted to make again. He'd cost her the freedom she held so dear. He wasn't anything special, at least Fake Nora didn't think so. He wasn't difficult to pretend to be, but his family had gotten suspicious almost as soon as she'd climbed out of the mirror. Jesse's sister especially. Fake Nora, back when she'd been The Other Jesse, had nearly starved trying to make the family fear. She needed them to let their guard down and trust she was their son.

They didn't.

And Fake Nora had paid for it by a painful trip through the mirror. She'd won in the end, though. They might have gotten rid of her, but they'd never gotten their precious jerk of a Jesse back.

And they wouldn't.

Fake Nora knew it wouldn't be long before Jesse would turn into a bad one. They all turned into bad ones, no matter how hard they fought against it.

So, what if Mr. Gibson knew, or thought he knew, something. It didn't mean anything. Nora's parents would never believe him if he told them. Everything would be okay as long as she stayed cool.

A few minutes later, Nora's mom drove them down the road, her purchases in the backseat, on the way to a new antique mall. Fake Nora laid her head against the seat and closed her eyes, thinking about all the things she needed to do to adapt to this life so things wouldn't turn out like it did the last time.

"Nora, everything okay?"

Fake Nora nodded, not wanting to talk.

"You've seemed strange since we left Gibson's. Did he say anything to you?"

Fake Nora shook her head.

"Good, 'cause as much as I like Mr. Gibson's store, he can be a bit different. He told me a story while I was paying about the mirror I bought last week. He said he should have told me then, and his conscience had berated him ever since. Can you believe that?"

In fact, she could.

"Do you want to hear the story? It's unreal. About some undead doppelgänger or something."

Doppelgänger. That's something she hadn't been called in a long time. A doppelgänger was a creature that could look like anyone, and then take over their lives. She supposed, if she wanted to be honest about things, she was a doppelgänger.

"Not really." She'd heard enough of the story from Mr. Gibson, not to mention the fact that she actually lived it.

It did raise a question, though. If Mr. Gibson told Nora's mother about the mirror, did that mean he believed it? Did Nora's mother believe it?

"Can we go home?" Fake Nora truly wanted to get out of the car and into her room. She needed to be alone to think all these things through. And being scared of Mr. Gibson had depleted some of her stored food. She would need Nora's brother to fill it up some more.

"You sure? We've only gone to two places. Are you sure there's nothing the matter with you?"

"I'm sure."

"And are you sure Mr. Gibson didn't say anything to upset you? Maybe about the mirror? Are you scared of it?"

Fake Nora glared at Nora's mother. "I'm not afraid of anything."

Nora's mother held up a hand in response. "Fine. I'll take you home."

"Thank you," Fake Nora said.

She meant it.

CHAPTER TWENTY-ONE

NORA

Nora ran as fast as she could down the hallway and into the guest room, closing the door behind her. She had no idea if closing that door kept the bad ones away like it did in the bathroom, but she didn't want to chance it. Knowing Fake Nora would be out shopping with her mother for a while, Nora raced to the mirror and threw the comforter off. She took a second to look at the mirror to see what reflected at her. Same as before. Everything was in the right place except her. She didn't see herself in the mirror because she didn't have a reflection. She was a reflection.

"Nolan!" Nora yelled as loudly as she could. She waited a second before yelling his name once more, hoping he'd hear her. "Nolan! It's me! It's Nora, your sister! Your real sister!"

She thought about pounding on the glass to get his attention. Touching the glass was an unknown, an unknown she didn't want to risk. What if she got stuck somewhere she didn't want to get stuck, worse than where she already was?

There was no movement in the doorway, which was where Nolan would have to come from. "Nolan, please! Come in here. It's me! It's Nora."

Still no movement. Nora felt her insides nearly burst with sadness. Why didn't he hear her? Why hadn't he come running after her? This was her one plan, her one plan to get out of there. Why wasn't he coming?

"Nolan!" She pounded on the dresser, careful not to touch the glass mirror. "Nolan, come in the guest room! I'm here, Nolan! I'm here!"

Nora pounded on the dresser one more time before falling to her knees, sobs erupting from her, shaking her entire body. This had been her last hope. It looked like Jesse was right. There was no way out. If she couldn't get the real world to hear her, except Fake Nora, who had been waiting for her, then they were truly stuck, waiting to turn into what all reflections turned into—the bad ones.

She'd never go home. Never see her mother again or her father. Never annoy Nolan.

Sobs shook her body as tears dripped off her nose. It wasn't fair. None of this was fair.

She wanted …

"Nora?" Nolan's voice filled her ears, and Nora stood to gaze into the mirror. Sure enough, Nolan stood there in all his five-year-old glory, right next to the mirror. He reached his hand out to touch the glass …

"No! Nolan, don't touch the mirror, okay? Don't touch it. I don't know what will happen to you if you touch it. And I don't want you stuck in here like me." Tears fell down Nora's cheeks, this time from happiness. He'd heard her! There was hope, maybe the smallest, tiniest amount of hope, but hope.

"Okay." He stepped back and put his hands in the air. "How did she get you in the mirror?"

"She? So, you know I'm not me? I mean, you know that the person with you isn't me?"

"Of course, I know, silly. I know my own sister."

If Nora could hug him, she would. "Good, that's good. I've never been so happy to see you in my life."

"Same. It's not the same without you here. The other you, she's not nice."

Anger built up in Nora. "Is she hurting you?"

"Not like that. No bruises. She keeps scaring me, doing all these things to make me afraid of her, and I am, Nora. I'm afraid of her. I try not to be, but I can't help it. She's scary."

Nora's heart broke from her little brother having to deal with so much. "I'm sorry, buddy. I'm sorry she's doing all this to you, but I have a plan."

His little eyes lit up. "You do? You're coming back home!"

"I hope so."

"And we can finish our soccer game?" he asked hopefully.

Her heart broke some more. "Yes, we will finish our game. But, in order to do it, I need your help."

"What can I do?" Nolan squared his shoulders.

"You can—" Nora's words were cut off by her mother yelling for Nolan. What were they doing home so soon? Fake Nora couldn't see her talking to Nolan. It would ruin the entire plan. "She's back! You have to hurry, but listen to me. Listen carefully. You cannot be afraid of her, okay? I need you to be brave and not be afraid."

"Why?" he asked innocently.

"Because it's important. She feeds on fear."

"She told me. That's why she keeps me afraid."

That settled it. Nora would do everything in her power to destroy Fake Nora. It was one thing to go after Nora; it was another to go after a little boy. "Then you can't let her feed off your fear, and to do that, you can't be afraid. And you can't tell her that you talked to me. She can't know. I'm working on something over here. If she finds out, I'll be stuck here forever."

"I don't want you stuck there forever." Nolan pouted.

"Me either, buddy."

"Nolan!" her mother called up the stairs. It felt so strange to hear an echo. Fake Nora would be coming up the stairs any minute.

"Remember, Nolan, don't be afraid of her, but you can't do it all at once. You need to be subtle."

"I don't know what that means. I'm five."

Nora winced. "Just, just try not to be afraid of her. Try a little each day until you aren't afraid of her anymore. Promise me, okay? Promise me, and I'll get back to you."

"I promise." He smiled brightly. "I'm happy to see you. I'm glad you are okay. She said if I tried to tell Mama and Daddy about her not being you, she'd hurt you." A small tear slid down his cheek, and he wiped it away angrily. "I didn't want to hurt you, so I didn't tell."

"I know, Nolan, and it's okay. I'm going to get out of here, I promise. With your help, I promise. Now, go."

Nolan ran toward the door, and with one final look behind him, ran down the hallway. Nora saw a shadow coming up the stairs. She had no idea if it was her mother or Fake Nora. If it was her mother, she could yell at her for help. If it was Fake Nora, she would know something was up and might hurt Nolan. She couldn't chance it, even if it was a fifty-fifty chance that it would be her mother and her mother could get her out. Nolan would help. He was all they had.

Determined, Nora quickly covered the mirror with the comforter, ran to the light switch, turned it off, and shut the door before anyone could see the weird reflection at her house.

The calls of her name started almost immediately. The calls and the wind rushing past her legs made her run toward the bathroom. The bad ones knew she was out and about. They weren't happy about it, either. With no time to waste, Nora nearly slammed into the bathroom and locked the door behind her. "I did it," she said breathlessly to Jesse. "I did it."

Jesse didn't answer her outright. He was talking, though. Talking and mumbling to himself. "Jesse?"

Nora slowly kept her eyes on the mirror as she walked toward the mirror and peeked inside. Jesse paced the floor, back and forth, quickly. His hands were in his pockets, then out of his pockets, in his hair, out of his hair. His movements were erratic. Words Nora couldn't understand were coming from his mouth, and he kept mumbling ... kept mumbling.

"Jesse?" she asked again. He was trying his best not to turn into a bad one. She could feel it.

He stopped pacing and looked up at her, his eyes red. Beads of sweat poured down his face. "I'm trying," Jesse whispered.

"I know. Try a little longer. I talked to Nolan. He's going to help us."

"Great ... my existence depends on a five-year-old." He scoffed lightly.

"Could be worse." She didn't see how, but there was always a worse option in her mind.

"Keep thinking that, Sunshine." He sounded sincere. With a quick nod, he turned his back to the mirror and started pacing and talking to himself once more.

Nora slid down to the floor and hugged her knees, unable to watch Jesse's turmoil in the mirror. He said she saw the positive in things. She hoped she did in this situation. Jesse was holding on because she asked him to, because she gave him hope.

She hoped it wasn't all in vain.

CHAPTER TWENTY-TWO

FAKE NORA

Fake Nora stood at the top of the steps, watching Nora's brother run down the hallway and into his room. She didn't know where he'd originated, but she had a sneaking suspicion it was either Nora's room or the guest room. Either way, he never would figure out how Fake Nora switched places with Nora.

The man from the store, however …

"Go lie down, honey. I'll check on you later." Nora's mother called from the bottom of the steps.

Fake Nora turned and nodded, exhausted. The trip out, even if it had only been two stores, nearly drained her. Not that she was hungry. She wasn't. But she was mentally drained. Here, she thought she was free, and then Mr. Gibson happened.

She couldn't get a good read on him, which angered her. She was always good at reading people. That's how she became so good at mimicking people, except for Jesse. People never saw through her, never questioned her, because she had been an amazing actress, and really, that's all taking over someone else's life was, acting like them. It was a game, in a way. A game to eat, of course, but a game nonetheless.

Fake Nora checked on Nora's brother before going to her room. He sat, like always, on his bed with his head covered up. "You ran down the hall very fast," she said, enjoying the fear snack he gave her.

"I heard you coming. Didn't want to see you," he admitted, much to Fake Nora's delight. At the end of the day, everything wasn't terrible. She had Nora's brother to feed her. She had a roof over her head. She wasn't trapped in that mirror. And if worse came to worst and Mr. Gibson somehow told Nora's mother about what was really happening … and if—and it was a big if—Nora's mother believed him, Fake Nora would simply leave. Easy as that. She would leave, make a new life for herself. People left all the time, at least they had in her day. It wouldn't be too difficult.

If the worst—worst—happened, then Fake Nora could always abandon the Nora identity and jump back into another mirror. As long as the mirror she jumped in wasn't covered, she could still jump out of another one. It was one of the stipulations she'd been given when she was still human by the person who cursed her to live in reflections. Anyway, it was a gamble because she didn't like to leave things to chance. It was a gamble to go into a mirror and find someone looking in another mirror at the exact same time to change lives with. It wasn't impossible, though, so if she had to do it … she would.

But, in Fake Nora's mind, she never saw that happening. Nora's brother was too scared of her to say anything. Nora's parents were too … much like parents … to believe that whatever happened with their family was not normal. A reflection taking over their kids' lives wasn't normal; therefore, they wouldn't believe it.

Still, Fake Nora's mind raced. She needed to lie down and steady her nerves. Leaving Nora's brother alone, Fake Nora went to Nora's bed, turned her back to the door, and looked out the window at the beautiful day. That was what she hated about Reflection World the most, how muted the sunshine was. How nothing ever felt like anything. Here, things could be felt, birds tweeted, the warm wind blew. Fake Nora relaxed, keeping her eyes trained outside the window, feeling, watching, enjoying. Soon she felt calm and allowed the outside world to lull her to sleep. Everything would be okay.

Everything would work out in her favor.

CHAPTER TWENTY-THREE

NORA

The fact that time meant nothing in the mirror world didn't mean that it didn't move slowly. Especially while waiting on Nolan to do his thing and starve Fake Nora. The plan was simple, which meant so many things could go wrong. All Fake Nora had to do was starve and disappear, then theoretically, everything would go back to normal.

The question was, how long would that take?

What if Fake Nora escaped ...?

What if she hurt Nolan ... ?

And the thing that bothered Nora at the moment was, what if Jesse couldn't hold on that long?

He'd been pacing for what seemed like hours, if time had meaning. He paced and mumbled, said things Nora couldn't understand. He talked about his family, about his little sister, Abigail, that he missed the most because they played together all the time. He talked about life on the farm, the war, being afraid …

Nora's heart broke when he talked about being afraid.

"Jesse?" Nora asked when she hadn't heard him in a while.

He didn't answer, which scared her. She jumped off the floor and looked in the mirror. He was standing still, his back to her, breathing heavily. Her heart nearly leaped out of her chest. She couldn't lose him! Not like this. "Jesse, hold on, okay? Hold on! We'll get you out. I promise! I promise."

"I can't, Sunshine." His voice was low and sad. "I can't fight it any longer."

Nora beat the sink. "Yes, you can! You can. Fight it, Jesse. Fight!"

When he didn't say anything, Nora didn't even think. Her time was up. Nolan's time was up. They needed to defeat Fake Nora now! She only hoped that he'd starved her enough to make her weak. At the very least, they needed her weak.

"Just a little bit longer. Hold on for me, Jesse, please!"

He looked up at her; his hands already started to fade.

"If you can get out of here, get out. Don't come back for me. Go back to your family." His arms faded more.

"No!" Nora raced out the door, not caring about the bad ones lurking in the hallway. She ran to the guest room, locked the door behind her, ripped the comforter from the mirror, and yelled for Nolan. She didn't care if Fake Nora heard her or not. Time was up, and she couldn't wait anymore.

"Nolan! Come here!" It was dark in the room, so it had to be nighttime in the real world. Everyone would be asleep, and Nolan was the deepest sleeper she ever heard. Nora pounded on the dresser. "Nolan! It's me! I need your help! Nolan!"

She banged harder and harder on the dresser, praying that Jesse hadn't turned into a bad one yet. Just a little more time … a little more time!

A shadow appeared in the doorway in the real world.

Then a light flickered on.

It was Fake Nora, rubbing her eyes. "Nora, you have a lot of nerve. I told you what would happen if you tried to get out. I told you what would happen to Nolan."

Nora hated to admit it, but she'd forgotten about it. She only wanted Jesse to be safe, and yes, Nolan, too, but she couldn't dwell on that now. She'd started this. She had to finish it.

All she had to do was get Fake Nora to the mirror, then maybe reach out and drag her into the mirror with her? Would that do any good? Nora had no idea. She was flying by the seat of her pants. Still, she tried …

"I need to talk to you." Nora changed her strategy.

"Then why were you calling for your brother?" Fake Nora stood in the doorway. No, she needed to walk closer to the mirror.

"I … I needed to see him. I got afraid, and I wanted to see something from the real world. The bad ones are after me." Nothing about that statement was a lie.

Fake Nora laughed darkly. "They do that, don't they? Come after you when you aren't expecting it. Poor things."

"'Poor things?' You put them here. You made them!" All the frustration, anger, sadness she'd had since Fake Nora had stolen her life bled out of her. She shook as she spoke, holding onto the dresser to keep her steady.

"I did make them." Fake Nora shrugged. "But so I could live. You have no idea what it's like to be shoved in a mirror as a punishment. Do you know my crime? I dared to gaze at my reflection too often. That was it! That ... and I killed one of the priests in town ... but mainly because of the looking in a mirror. My mother feared retribution from the town, and she said she did it for my own good. She said she hid me away in a mirror so they could never get me, never kill me. And I hated that world. It was worse than being dead, so I figured a way out of it."

As she spoke so passionately, Fake Nora walked toward the mirror. "I had to adapt to survive. My time in the mirror made human food turn my stomach, but fear filled me up. I changed. I adapted. And here I am, the person you see now."

"All I see is me," Nora said, trying to anger her more. It seemed that when Fake Nora was mad, she lost all sense of herself. She made mistakes, and that's what Nora needed, for Fake Nora to make a mistake.

"And all I see is a reflection who can't get into the real world and never will." Fake Nora stood inches from the dresser. She was so close Nora could reach out and touch her. She didn't know if she could, but she would try. She'd do anything to save Jesse, save Nolan, save them all.

"Maybe. Maybe I'll spend the rest of my days here. Maybe I'll become a bad one, too, but no matter what, you'll never be me. Never. Nolan already knows. Soon, everyone else will know, too."

"They won't believe him." Fake Nora slammed her hands on the dresser. This was it. This was Nora's chance.

"Maybe they won't have to." Nora reached up to grab Fake Nora when, from the corner of her eye, she saw Nolan, little Nolan, come running into the room. He ran up behind Fake Nora and gave her a shove into the mirror.

Fake Nora screamed as, instead of the glass breaking, she was shoved into the reflection world, right on top of Nora. Both Noras fell in a heap on the floor. Nora stood, as did Fake Nora. Nolan breathed heavily from the other side of the mirror.

It was easy to tell the two Noras apart. Nora had on the clothes she'd been wearing the entire time she'd been in Reflection World. And Fake Nora had on Nora's pajamas, the ones with unicorns she loved so well.

"You little ..." Fake Nora ran toward the mirror, toward Nolan. Nora grabbed Fake Nora around the waist and dragged her backwards. She wouldn't get her brother. She'd never get out of this place. Nora might not, either, but at the very least, she'd know Fake Nora would never hurt anyone ever again.

From behind the locked door, she heard them: the bad ones. Wind rushed like a hurricane outside. Screams and snarls erupted as if they knew what had happened: the one who had caused them to be here was back, and she was vulnerable. They wanted her, and Nora was obliged to give her to them.

"Don't do this!" Fake Nora screamed, scratching at Nora's eyes, her face, anything she could reach. "Don't! You don't know what you're doing!"

"No, you didn't know what you were doing when you messed with me," Nora growled. In one swift motion, Nora held onto Fake Nora with one hand, unlocked the door with the other, and opened it. Fake Nora wriggled out of Nora's grasp and ran toward the mirror, ran toward Nolan! She was already changing forms, from Nora into a small five-year-old boy. She was going to switch places with Nolan.

Not hesitating, Nora grabbed Fake Nora by the shirt, a white one just as Nolan wore, and dragged her to the door. Once there, she flung her out to where the bad ones were waiting. Nora slammed the door and held it with her back, hearing the tearing, the screaming, the gnashing of teeth as the bad ones got their revenge on Fake Nora … or whatever her real name was.

"Nora!" Nolan called from the other side of the mirror. If Fake Nora could get through one way, she could get through the other way.

But one thing was left. She had to go get Jesse. She had to …

"Nora, come on!" Nolan screamed.

But Nora couldn't go without Jesse. He'd been her friend since all this started. Even with the horrible sounds in the hallway, Nora steeled her nerves and made up her mind. With one last look at Nolan, Nora ran out the door, through the wind, through the blood, through the screams, through her parent's wedding pictures falling off the wall and nearly hitting her.

She ran to the mirror in the bathroom. "Jesse, I did it!" She froze. The mirror was empty. "Jesse …"

Her heart sank. She'd been too late. He'd already turned.

She wiped a tear as she turned toward the door and back to her brother.

"Nora …" A small, pained voice came through

the mirror. Nora went back quickly to see Jesse crawling toward the mirror from one of the back rooms. "I didn't give up, but I can't hold on … much longer …"

"You don't have to. She's dead."

Jesse stopped crawling. "She's … she's dead? How?"

"The bad ones killed her." Nora tore the shower curtain from the tub. "Stand back. I'm getting you out of there, then we're going home."

Jesse covered his eyes as Nora shattered the mirror. As she did, the house rumbled under her. If Reflection World was like Fake Nora's prison of sorts, now that she was dead, there was no need for it, and … it was collapsing.

They needed out. Fast!

With the mirror gone, Jesse fell out of the frame and into Nora's arms. He hugged her tightly, tighter than anyone had ever hugged her in her life. "We have to go," she reminded him, hugging him back. "Can you walk?"

"I might need some help." He looked down, and he was still fading. Why? Why was he fading when Fake Nora was dead?

It didn't matter. They were getting out. "We're

going back to my guest room. Nolan is there. He'll pull us out, okay?"

Jesse nodded. Nora put Jesse's arm over her shoulder as she opened the door to the hallway.

The hallway looked like a movie set, one of those disaster movies. There was debris everywhere, blood. The bad ones swirled around as the house rumbled under them like an earthquake or a sink-hole would swallow them all.

Jesse hung onto her as they ran toward the guest room. A piece of the ceiling fell behind them with a crash, causing the bad ones to swirl wildly. They were going to make it, though. They were so close! So close!

Nora opened the door to the guest room as another chunk of ceiling fell behind her. She dragged Jesse through the door and toward the mirror where Nolan waited, his eyes wide. He was watching what was happening in the mirror, and it had to terrify him. It terrified Nora, and she was much older.

"Almost there," she told Jesse. Almost there!

She dragged Jesse through the room. With each step, they were closer and closer to freedom. So close …

Another earthquake rocked the house, sending

the foundation crumbling. Nora felt the floor give way as she and Jesse started falling toward the ground, along with everything else in the room. They were falling … falling … house, the room, the dresser.

Nora clung to Jesse as they fell down. When she looked above her, the mirror came down as well. The last thing she saw was Nolan reaching for her.

Then the crash.

And everything went black.

CHAPTER TWENTY-FOUR

NORA

It felt like a dream.

A strange dream like from the Wizard of Oz where Dorothy Gale is convinced that her family was a lion, a tin man, and a scarecrow. That's how everything felt to Nora. Surreal.

Like what happened to her hadn't happened, but she knew it had.

It hadn't been a dream.

She sat up from bed with a start, looking all over the room to see where she was. It looked like her room, all right. Same bed. Same curtains. Same everything. Then again, her bed in the reflection world looked the same, too.

"Shhhh … it's okay," Nora's mother said beside her.

Her mother! Her actual mother!

Nora almost couldn't believe it. She grabbed her mom and held her tightly, never wanting to let her go. "It's you! It's really you!" Nora buried her face in her mother's hair, smelling the familiar lavender shampoo as tears fell down her face.

"Of course, it's me, Nora. Who else would it be?"

So many people … so many.

"What happened? What day is it?"

"Saturday, like it's been all day. What's gotten into you?" Her mother pushed some hair behind Nora's ear. She looked concerned, and Nora didn't want to worry her anymore. "Just a weird dream, that's all." Even though Nora knew for a fact, it wasn't a dream.

"Weird things have gone on for a while now." Her mother sighed. "I got up this morning, and the beautiful antique dresser in the guest room was lying down, and the glass shattered."

Nora never wanted to do a happy dance so much in her life. It was gone! It was over! "That's terrible."

"It is. I thought it was a beautiful piece. Now no one will ever get to enjoy it again."

And Nora was incredibly happy about that.

She looked around the room then, wondering what in the world had happened to Jesse. He got out, right? He was fine …

"I don't suppose you want to go antique shopping with me today, do you?"

It took a second for the question to register with Nora. "Yes, why wouldn't I?"

Her mom shrugged a bit sadly. "I don't know. Last week, you seemed done with it. I thought maybe you'd grown out of it."

Nora hugged her mom tightly. "I haven't grown out of anything. I'd love to go with you. Just let me get dressed."

"Good luck with that." Her mom said as Nora gathered her clothes. "The mirror in the bathroom is broken, too, shattered on the floor. Took me forever to clean it all up, so be careful in case I missed some of the little shards. Don't want them to get stuck in your foot."

Surely, that meant Jesse had gotten out too, right? "Thanks. I'll be careful."

When she got to the door, her mother had one last thing to ask, "Nora, do you know anything about the broken mirrors?"

"Not a thing, Mama. Not a thing."

On the way to the bathroom, Nora swung by

Nolan's room. He was hiding under his covers, so Nora slid under them, too. He backed away slightly when he saw her, then he narrowed his eyes. "Nora?"

She nodded, and Nolan pulled her into a big hug. She even took the opportunity to kiss him on top of the head. He deserved it. "You did it, kid. You saved us."

"I did what you said. I didn't fear her. I didn't feed her. She tried everything, and I wasn't afraid."

"You weakened her enough for me to defeat her. Good job!" She ruffled his hair. "Nothing to be afraid of now."

"Nothing," he repeated.

"Hey, what happened with the other boy?"

"Other boy?" Nolan's brows knitted together.

"Yeah, Jesse. The one I came through the mirror with."

Nolan shook his head. "Only one person came through the mirror, Nora. And that was you."

Nora's heart sank as she realized what had happened. Jesse hadn't come through the mirror with her. She hadn't saved Jesse after all.

"I'm sorry you're sad," Nolan said, snuggling up to Nora.

"I'm not sad." Nora hugged her brother tightly.

She was sad about Jesse, but she didn't want him to know it. This was a happy day. She was home.

She was home.

After hugging her brother a few minutes more, Nora went into the bathroom with the broken mirror and stared where the frame hung with no glass inside. Jesse was gone.

It was then that she allowed herself time to mourn and feel all the things she'd been through in the last two weeks, away from home.

She brushed her teeth, washed her face, and thought about Jesse, wondering where he was now and if he was okay.

CHAPTER TWENTY-FIVE

NORA

Nora's mother pulled into the gravel parking lot of Gibson's Antiques and shut off the ignition. "I've been here two weeks in a row. I'm not sure I want to go back. And he was a little odd last week, talking about that mirror. I don't know."

"I want to go in. Since we are already here." Nora looked at the building, not impressive in the least, but it had given her the adventure, and the scare, of a lifetime. It made her appreciate the time she had with her family and her friends.

"Okay, then." Her mother nodded, and off they went.

Once inside, as normal, her mother went one way, and Nora went the other way. She meandered around the store until she came to the small back hallway where the mirror had been two weeks ago. Nora wished she'd never gone back there on that day. Then again, if she hadn't, she wouldn't have met Jesse, and even though she'd never see him again, she was grateful for the time she knew him. She hoped, wherever he was, he was happy.

"Nothing back here that'll interest a thing like you," a male voice said curtly behind her.

Nora turned, confused. A thing like her? It was Mr. Gibson, the owner. She remembered him from the day he sold them the mirror. At first, his eyes were hard, then they eased up, and a smile pulled on his lips. "You're you again," he said in disbelief.

"I'm me." She beamed. It was nice to know someone noticed Fake Nora wasn't her, even if it was a man who owned the store. "How did you know she wasn't me?"

"I could tell. I regretted selling you that mirror ever since I did it, and my ma, she raked me over the coals for it. Said I never should have done it, and that I'd cursed you. But you made it out. You made it!" He patted her on the head, which Nora appreciated. A hug from him might have been a little much.

"Is your ma, I mean, was she kin to a boy named Jesse?" 'Cause if she was, Nora knew it was her obligation to tell her about how Jesse fought bravely and how he never gave up.

Mr. Gibson looked down at the floor. "I think you need to come with me."

"Why?"

"Just … I know Ma would love to talk to you."

Nora hated to tell Mr. Gibson that she wasn't going anywhere without her mother. And then, an old woman's voice came behind him. "Don't scare the girl, Teddy. She's been through enough."

An older woman who had to be in her late eighties, leaned on a doorway, which stood where the hallway and the store met. She had a cane in one hand and a biscuit in the other. Her white hair was placed in a bun on top of her head. Silver glasses barely stayed on her nose. "My name is Abigail."

"Abigail? As in Jesse's sister, Abigail?"

The old woman nodded.

Nora felt her legs give way, but she wouldn't allow herself to faint. She had one last job to do, for Jesse. He'd fought for her, and she'd fight for him.

She took a step closer to Miss Abigail. "Ma'am. I'm sorry to be the one to tell you this, but your brother, Jesse, he's …"

"Right here."

Nora turned, and, from behind Miss Abigail,

Jesse's hand raised. It was as young as ever. It couldn't be true … how could it be true?

"Jess—Jesse?" Nora croaked, nearly falling over herself to get to him. Miss Abigail grinned from ear to ear as she moved out of the way for Jesse to get to Nora.

Jesse, who was still his thirteen-year-old self, picked up Nora and swung her around in circles.

They'd done it!

They were both out of the mirror. They were both alive!

"How?" she whispered in his ear. He stopped spinning her, but he hadn't put her feet down on the floor.

"I don't know. I woke up in this store. I didn't recognize it at first. And you weren't here. I thought … I thought you were gone."

"I thought *you* were gone." She hugged him tighter around the neck.

"This store, this house," Miss Abigail began. "Was my family's house way back in the forties."

Nora leaned back and looked at Jesse's face. "This was your home?"

He nodded. "This was my home. And you got me back to it. I can never thank you enough."

Jesse sat her down on the floor, took her hand,

and led her to Miss Abigail, hugging his sister around the neck with one arm and holding Nora's hand with the other. "My baby sister, older than me now."

"Nah, you're still the oldest. I'm just the prettiest," Miss Abigail replied lightly. "I can't thank you enough for bringing Jesse back to me. I always had him with the mirror, but I wasn't sure how to get him out, and my father made me promise to never remove the cover. But Teddy, here, he didn't believe me about my brother or the curse or the doppelgänger who lived in the mirror and drank fear."

Nora believed. She believed whole-heartedly. "Glad I could help. And Jesse helped me, too. In the mirror world. He helped save us both."

"I'm so glad to have my brother back." Miss Abigail pressed her aging lips to Jesse's cheek. "So glad."

"Um … what's going on here?" Nora's mother asked, holding a few plates in her hands.

"Family reunion," Nora answered, gripping Jesse's hand tighter. "A family reunion."

ACKNOWLEDGMENTS

I want to thank Mary and Cammie at Monster Ivy Publishing for believing in this book (and me). This is our third book together! I can't believe it. Time has flown by.

I also want to thank all the kids who have read WHAT RACHEL DID and told me how much they loved it. And a huge shout out to their parents who told me how it freaked their kids out ... in a good way. I know you've been waiting a year for another MG book from me. Here you go!

Special thanks to my family for being with me through the last nine years of my publishing life. It means a lot, and I know it's not easy at times.

Thank you to God for everything.

Thank you to YOU! You mean more to me than you know!

ABOUT THE AUTHOR

Kelly Martin lives in a possibly haunted house in a small Southern town. While she'd like to say paranormal things have only happened to her at her home, it would be a lie.

She is an active member of the Horror Writers Association and an international #1 best selling author in horror, paranormal, contemporary, historical, young adult, and mysteries. All of Kelly's books have one thing in common—imagine the real world is tilted slightly on its side. You don't really know what's going on, what's missing, but there is a tilt, a hum you can barely hear, telling you that something is off.

Email Kelly Martin at kelly@kellymartinbooks.com (no spaces).

Want to know about new releases, chat with Kelly, go behind the scenes on all her books? Find out how here: https://linktr.ee/kellymartinauthor.

Keep your ghostly adventure going with *Dark*

and Deadly Things (book 1 in the Haunted House series). Full series out now.

ALSO BY KELLY MARTIN

YA Inspirational

CROSSING THE DEEP

BIG IS BEAUTIFUL

Paranormal

DARK AND DEADLY THINGS SERIES

HEARTLESS SERIES

BETWEEN THE DREAMING AND THE DEAD

THE AFTERLIFE OF LIZZIE MONROE

TRINITY ROW

WHAT RACHEL DID

WHAT RACHEL DID

WHAT RACHEL DID

Jacob Mosley died twenty years ago. His creepy old house has sat abandoned ever since.

At least that's what my best friend, Bradley's, Mom told him, and he told me since he'd lived in White's Chapel all his life. I moved in at six years old.

Everyone had a different take on Jacob Mosley's demise, though. Lots of different rumors. I chose to believe Bradley's version, since his Mom was a nurse and in the hospital the day they brought in dead Old Man Mosley.

The Mosley Manor (as we called it), a two-story fixer-upper that had probably been white at one time, maybe even pretty—not that it is anymore—was the local ghost story. The house that people dared each other to enter on Halloween. The one that sat ominously smack in the middle of town, surrounded by a browning yard, falling wooden fence, and grass that sways in even the slightest breeze. The one with the new "For Sale!" sign sitting in the front yard: the only new thing to touch the house since who knows when? Probably since the ambulance that hauled poor Old Man Mosley away.

I slowed in front of Mosley Manor on the way home from school, as I did every day, and as Bradley did every day, he kept right on going. "Scaredy cat!" I yelled after him with a laugh. I knew why everyone else was afraid of Mosley Manor. I didn't understand why Bradley was.

My best friend since … forever … Bradley was a lot like me: intellectual, big on facts, and lover of all things scientific and historical and proven.

The only thing one could prove about Mosley Manor was that the grass needed mowing, and the nails discarded around the property probably contributed to tetanus if you were unlucky enough to step on one.

But Bradley was terrified of the place. So scared that he'd actually tried to convince me, on several occasions, to ride our bikes home another way: a way that wasn't a straight shot from school. One that didn't go directly by Mosley Manor.

I, the nice friend I am, told him there was nothing to worry about and refused to let fear hurt my friend.

Not all twelve-year-olds are as nice as I am.

Not sure Bradley considers it nice.

Tough love, I suppose.

"Hey, Bradley! Hold up!" He'd nearly passed the large oak tree that should have been cut down years ago for how badly it was messing up the side-walk. His head lulled forward, probably contemplating how he got lucky enough to have me as a best friend. Finally, as I knew he would, he put on his brakes and looked back at me.

"I'm not going in there!" he yelled back.

"I would never ask you to." Though I would ask him to, if not to get rid of his silly fear of the place. It was just a house. Just like our houses, which sat next to each other. Just a house … just a house.

The white curtain fluttered in the upstairs window.

"What do you want?" he asked, a bit miffed.

I took my eyes from the house. My rational mind already decided it had been a mouse running by the curtain to make it move.

"The for sale sign is new." I pointed to it, knowing that he would never have seen it himself. He probably rode by the place with his eyes closed.

"Good. Maybe whoever buys it will tear it down. Put up a parking lot or something." As he spoke, he took the time to look up and down the house. The longer he looked, the bigger his eyes became. I was glad he didn't see the curtain move. He wouldn't be rational like me. He would probably jump and run, scream like a scared chicken, and embarrass himself when I finally caught up with him.

"Better not let the house hear you say that." I pushed the pedals of my bike to begin rolling toward him. "You know what they say about ghosts. They listen."

He shivered as I passed him, which gave me a small sort of satisfaction. Chess, Bradley could beat me in. Website design, he was a natural. This house … my win.

"Thought you didn't believe in ghosts," he huffed as he rode up beside me. Even though he complained, I knew he was happy to be riding away from the house. If a crow cawed, it would have made my life.

"I don't. Doesn't mean they don't believe in me." I winked as I pedaled faster, leaving him in the dust.

Ten minutes later, we pulled into my driveway. Our houses were a lot alike: two-story, white. His had black shutters where mine were gray. His house had one car in front of it: a blue Kia. It was his Mom's, and she had nearly paid it off, or so she kept saying. My house had a white four-door truck (my dad's) and a silver Challenger (my mom's). There was a basketball goal over my garage, which had belonged to the people who'd lived there before us and that my dad never thought about taking down. My little brother's bike lay like a lump in the yard. Mom picked him up from school every day. She didn't trust him to make it home like she trusted Bradley and me. Course, my brother being eight probably had a lot to do with it, too.

Bradley had no siblings. It was just him and his mom and had been since his dad died. It was sad, but if that hadn't happened, I never would have met Bradley. His dad died when Bradley was a baby. His Mom bought the house next to mine. A few years later, we rented ours. My parents had been talking about owning a house, their very own house, for years, but I didn't think it would ever happen. I didn't want it to happen, to be frank. I loved our house. I loved living next to Bradley.

Anyway, we'd been best friends ever since. The

older we got, people at school teased us about being boyfriend and girlfriend—namely Gracie, who for some reason came up with my stupid nickname ("Dorkland" ... a play on my last name, Kirkland. I wasn't even a dork. I was more of a nerd. Not that Gracie would know the difference ...) Anyway, no matter what Gracie said, Bradley wasn't my boyfriend. Nothing was further from the truth.

Bradley had been my friend through thick and thin over the last six years. We were neighbors. We were inseparable. We were—

"Ava! I'm glad you're home!" my mother yelled from the porch. "I have amazing news! We just bought the Mosley place! We will finally be homeowners!"

Bradley wobbled back a bit, catching himself on his bike for support. I looked at him. His face had turned an ashy white. "M-Mosley Manor? With the g-ghosts?"

This wasn't good.

Not good at all.

CPSIA information can be obtained
at www.ICGtesting.com
Printed in the USA
FSHW021302010321
79061FS